I0719738

THE SHERIFF'S

JACOB'S REDEMTPION

DREAM

ARTHUR KASPER

Contents

Book 3

It is the Soviet Union that runs against the tide of human history by denying human freedom and human dignity to its citizens.
The Soviet Union is the focus of evil in the modern world.

—President Ronald Reagan

"But what is happiness except the simple harmony between a (person) and the life the (person) leads?"

Albert Camus, Nobel Prize winning author

# Prologue

For the past twenty-four hours, two men, one of whom was a Catholic priest, dodged bullets between the trees while evading the Polish secret police. Running almost the entire time, they rested only briefly so they could maintain their slim lead.

The hunters had been ordered by the KGB to kill the priest.

One could almost sense the odor of death in the air of Poland. Oppressiveness draped the country like a wet piece of cheesecloth.

Several Catholic priests had been murdered in Poland since World War II by the secret police on orders from the USSR-appointed Communist leaders of the country secretly installed by the dictator Josef Stalin, premier of the Union of Soviet Socialist Republics.

It was 1980—somewhere in one of Poland's many beautiful forests not far from the Baltic Sea coast.

The early-fall weather was nasty. Occasionally the sunlight would break through small openings between the branches and the foliage. The heavy July rain forcefully struck them, sometimes holding them back. The trees were devoid of game birds. There was a musty odor in the air that bothered the priest, but he tried to ignore it. Once in a while he would see a bird or two flitting among the trees. The lush pine forest was so dense he felt sure his pursuers would not see him until they were close, and so he tried to listen for the noise they made rushing through the trees.

This particular Polish area consisted of peat bogs, marshes, lakes, and meadows where people loved to walk as they enjoyed nature. They might see wolves, wild boar, fox, deer, and elk.

When the rainwater soaked through their clothing, the two men felt so cold that they thought they might be hypothermic. But they kept running because moving made them feel warmer.

The police agents were close behind.

The shoes worn by the two fleeing men were heavy with mud; the water-soaked leaves made sucking sounds when the men pushed them into the muck, their legs churning like the hot pistons of a race car engine.

The priest barely heard his companion's voice over his own labored breathing even though Heinz was close behind him. Peter Heinz was an experienced guide escorting the priest through the unfamiliar forests.

"I can't go farther," gasped Heinz. "It's too painful to move my legs." His muscles burned from the stress and fatigue.

The priest told him, "You must go on. Otherwise they will kill you, and you don't want to die out here. Keep trying."

"No, Padre, I don't want to die."

The priest, who was six feet tall and 220 pounds of pure muscle—, the result of daily exercise—had dark brown eyes and reddish hair cut short in a military style. His companion, Heinz, was only five feet tall, weighing nearly three hundred pounds and afflicted with asthma aggravated by the foul weather, the stress of the activity, and the uncertainty of their fate.

The pursuers were closer than they had seemed the day before, and the priest thought the agents were gaining on them each day and could catch up with them in less than twenty-four hours.

The priest refused to stop. To do so meant the failure of his mission, and he had promised his Jesuit superior, Pope John Paul II, and US president Ronald Reagan that he would return from Poland with the intelligence on the activities of Solidarity, the union of Polish workers who were seeking freedom from the tyrannical Communist regime.

President Reagan was allied with the Polish pope to free the Poles from the oppressive Polish Communist government. Turning to Heinz, he recited the words from a Robert W. Service poem: "A promise made is a debt unpaid."

"Father!" shouted Heinz. "Please. We must stop. We must rest."

As the priest slowed and turned toward Heinz, he heard the sound of the two rifle shots, and then something hit the leaves. Another bullet slammed into the oak tree next to Heinz, and bits of bark stung his cold face like needles. Heinz faltered, lost his balance, and stumbled forward before tripping and falling facedown into the mud. He tried to stand. The priest helped, both men panting desperately for air.

"You can do it!" shouted the priest. He lifted Heinz's arm onto his aching shoulder and hoisted his companion. A smacking sound came from Heinz's back. He pitched forward into the mud. The priest struggled to stand, but he too fell into the mud. A vision of Christ falling under the weight of the cross flashed across the priest's mind. A bullet hit the beech tree where he had been standing. With the sound of paper tearing, another went over his head and into the open soggy denseness.

Heinz said nothing.

The priest said, "Talk to me."

Still Heinz said nothing.

The priest pulled the limp Heinz off the path and deeper into the heavy foliage. He crawled, dragging his companion underneath some shrubs. Feeling for a pulse, he searched but decided there was none. He heard the noise of the pursuers and saw them faintly in the dim distance. He said prayers over the dead man and removed his identification. He then covered the body with leaves and branches before fleeing deeper into the forest on the path he had abandoned.

The rain-soaked priest ran, dodging trees, tripping over branches, and falling breathlessly into the mud and leaves. He sensed that the Polish secret police agents were close and getting closer.

The priest got to his feet, looked back, and got a glimpse of his pursuers through the foliage. One of the agents fired his handgun, but the bullet missed the priest as he ran to the right and hid behind a tree. One of the pursuers moved closer, while the others continued on the pathway. When the pursuer came to the tree, the priest quickly grabbed him from behind and knocked him unconscious and then continued running through the forest.

After a short distance, the priest tripped when his right foot hit a thin hidden wire that ran ankle high across his path. He hit soggy ground with a mushy thud.

Three men rushed from the bushes and pulled him by his legs down an embankment and into a cave. They sat him in the back of the cave, and one of the group waited at the opening with his automatic rifle ready. He listened to the noise the pursuing agents made when they raced near the cave.

A short time later, the pursuers stopped. They breathed heavily as they looked around but saw nothing along the trees, bushes, rocks, and an occasional animal.

The female pursuer said, "Shit. Where could he have gone?"

"We cannot let him get away."

"He gets away, we are dead meat."

The man asked, "How could he just vanish?"

She answered, "It's the partisans. They live in the forest like animals." Inside the cave, one of them said, "Father, you are safe here. Say hello to your saviors, Hans and Helmut. I am Willi. You are Father Dumbowski, correct?"

"Yes," the priest answered.

Willi had small dark eyes and bushy hair that came over his forehead. He spoke with a slight speech impediment. "How did you know where I was?"

"We have been following you. Why were you on foot?" Willi asked.

The priest slouched in the rear of the cave and watched as Helmut carefully looked outside and then exited the cave into the darkness and the rain.

The priest answered, "Missed the last car."

"We are saddened by Heinz's death," Willi said. "Just as soon as it is safe, we will bury his body. Then we go to Rome. We have a rendezvous time."

Helmut asked. "Are you worried, Father?"

"I trust in God."

Hans asked, "So why do you risk your soft neck for us Poles?"

"To bring down an evil government."

Hans was a stocky middle-aged man with a week of growth on his face. "So you hate," he noted.

"I hate what they are doing."

"But you do not deny that you seek revenge."

The priest answered, "Revenge is God's business. Christ told us to love everyone—even our enemies."

Willi said, "I could never do that."

Father Dumbowski told him, "Then you are not a true Christian."

"Now love I believe in. If you weren't a priest, I'd say there was a woman involved somewhere."

The priest made a strong demand. "Now can we get out of here?"

"As soon as Hans says we can."

Just then, Helmut returned and announced, "It's quiet out there and time to leave."

The men exited the cave.

It was the last time anyone saw the priest alive.

Book 1

Poland's History of Turbulence

The history of Poland is a report of a thousand years of turbulence. During that time, three important Poles appeared on the world stage. Astronomer Nicolaus Copernicus was instrumental in establishing the concept of a heliocentric solar system, in which the sun, rather than the earth, is the center of the solar system. Considered Poland's greatest composer, Frédéric Chopin focused his efforts on piano composition and was a strong influence on composers who followed. Finally, Joseph Conrad, a Polish British writer, is regarded as one of the greatest novelists to write in the English language.

Two aggressive powers, Germany on the west and Russia on the east, wanted the country each for itself. This of course led to their struggling over it.

Poland had been the largest country in Europe during the seventeenth century, and there was a caste system in which the crown ruled, the clergy prayed, the burgers traded, the Jews were merchants, and the peasants were farmers working the fields.

By the start of the eighteenth century, Russia had strengthened its grip over Poland as Catherine the Great, empress of Russia, intervened in Poland's affairs. Russia, Prussia, and Austria then annexed 30 percent of Poland.

What was left of the country was the first partition in 1791 by Russia and eliminated what Catherine called a dangerous democracy. Russian troops were sent into Poland. In 1793 Russia and Prussia grabbed more than half the remaining Polish territory. A Polish armed rebellion in 1794 was defeated by the Russian troops. It was led by Tadeusz Kosciuszko, who had been a hero of the

American War of Independence. The third partition in 1795, created by the three occupying powers of Austria-Hungary, Germany, and Russia, divided Poland's territory among themselves. This resulted in Poland's disappearance from the map of Europe.

As early as the 1790s, Europeans viewed Poland's freedom as a conflict with its peace and felt that if Europe sliced up the country, the whole continent would be safer. After 1815, the lion's share of Poland territory was governed by the czar of Russia, who strangled Polish culture, including the language.

These events resulted in Poland rising up against Russia in 1830, with the effect of many Poles fleeing the country. Alexander, the Russian czar who created the Congress Kingdom of Poland, violated the laws of the country in the 1860s, which angered the Poles. They, in turn, staged anti-Russia demonstrations in Warsaw. As a result, the Poles, especially the Jews, were punished by the Cossacks.

In the 1870s, Russia more aggressively tried to eradicate Polish culture by suppressing Polish language, education, administration, and commerce, replacing them with the Russian way of doing business.

The Turks who respected the Poles told them they could rise to high positions in Turkey if they became Muslims, which many did. In 1886 Otto von Bismarck of Germany advocated buying out Polish landowners, which led to competitive farming. This, in turn, led to a large-scale emigration to the United States. By the outbreak in 1914 of World War I, four million Poles (from a population of about twenty- three million) had left the country with most of them sailing to America.

Most of the fighting during World War I took place on territories inhabited by the Poles who suffered staggering losses of life and livelihood. Germany and its ally Austria ended Russian occupation of Poland in 1915 as a result of its victory on the Eastern Front.

There was no Polish Army, and two million Poles conscripted into the Russian, German, and Austrian armies fought each other. Polish independence came about by the Russian Revolution in 1917, the final collapse of the Austrian Empire in October 1918, and the withdrawal of the German Army from Warsaw in November 1918.

Then Poland founded its second republic. The Polish country and economy were in ruins, and the country reemerged as a sovereign nation after World War I when it was recognized by the Allied governments, the victors of the war.

Thus began twenty-one years of Polish sovereignty, which was doomed tragically when Poland was devastated again during World War II. As a result, the country lost six million people, 18 percent of its population, by 1945, the end of the Second World War.

Poland has not perished yet as long as we Poles still live. That which foreign force has seized we at sword point shall retrieve.

—the first lines of the Polish national anthem

The narrator thought about the time he had been in Kenya. By chance, there had been nearby a film company focusing cameras on the predatory behavior of the lioness. They got as close as they dared to record on 35 mm film two animals tearing apart the carcass of a gazelle. The two lionesses paid no attention to the film crew.

As he observed the phenomenon—the natural lifecycle of the jungle—he conjured up in his mind the imagery of how Germany and the USSR, the two great powers of Europe, tore apart the defenseless country of Poland.

Thus came about this story of a Polish family who was caught up in the misfortunes of the roots of the war that took hold on August 23, 1939, when Germany and Stalinist USSR signed a nonaggression pact containing a secret protocol defining the partition of Eastern Europe.

The two countries planned to carve up the Polish state between themselves. Soviet Premier Joseph Stalin intended to create a Polish puppet state. And Adolph Hitler annexed his portion with Germany and made the central region thereof the so-called General

Government ruled by the Nazi attorney Hans Frank. He conducted business in the Wawel Castle in Kraków, which had been the original ancient capital and heart of Poland with its Catholic culture. This resulted in two Polands: the sword and the cross, the nation and the faith.

In violation of his agreement with Stalin notwithstanding, Hitler invaded Poland at dawn on Friday, September 1, 1939. The explosions began in Gdansk, formerly known in German as Danzig, a city that Hitler felt belonged to Germany, except it had been given to Poland by the 1918 Versailles Treaty that ended World War I and was meant to prevent the armament of Germany so the country would not begin another war.

The stubborn Polish resistors could only hold out one week against the shelling from the air and sea. The Nazi Luftwaffe flew medium two-engine bombers, the Heinkel HE 111, which, according to German propaganda, were actually civilian transports, and thus not forbidden by the Treaty of Versailles.

Stuka dive bombers released their deadly loads while nearly two million troops invaded Poland's borders from German-controlled territory. One week later, a contingent of them entered the city of Warsaw. Hitler's blitzkrieg by his modern German Army actually had been prohibited by the Treaty, but no nation moved to stop him. Thus, the German dictator easily overran the country with his formidable forbidden forces. The Polish citizens were so destitute they butchered horses killed by the bombing for meat.

Another German wave attacked Warsaw, which surrendered in twenty-seven days, during which time refugees loaded wagons and fled the city to the east while German planes shot anything that moved. The German blitzkrieg defeated the Polish Army in approximately six weeks. The displaced citizens watched the flames and smoke rising over the city and heard the explosions of the unexpected bombing. The winter weather of 1940/41 was so severe the people had no heat, and food was so scarce that prices increased daily. Refugees stayed under trees during the day and moved at night between burning buildings to avoid being shot by the Nazi Luftwaffe pilots.

On January 16, 1945, the Germans evacuated Warsaw and began their retreat to Germany. The Soviet military rolled into the city. They were allowed to be there by terms of the Yalta Conference, during which US president Franklin D. Roosevelt favored giving the Soviets all that Stalin wanted because his troops were helping to end the war. The United States also expected the USSR to help defeat the Japanese.

SS Obergruppenfuhrer
Heinrich Gropius, 1939

Casimir Gorska was preparing his Restauracja Polonia for the midday meals when the noise of Nazi boots reverberated from the Warsaw street paving stones bordering his building in Old Town Square. He stopped what he was doing and quickly went to look through a window where he saw the group of organized, fully armed, uniformed soldiers who were goose-stepping briskly and precisely along the street. He knew from the news reports that Gdansk was conquered by the Germans within a few days, and Poland's ammunition depots were destroyed.

Casimir was medium height with a robust stature and had a high forehead as a result of a receding black hairline. His brown eyes had people thinking he was kind and generous, which he was. His eyeglasses sat low on his nose. He had been born in Warsaw during the country's era of freedom and prosperity shortly after the end of World War I, in which his father was wounded and had recently died from natural causes. Casimir became popular in the city, which helped his success as one of the better restaurants located on the Warsaw Old Town Market Square not far from the Royal Castle.

His four-year-old son, Jacob, was playing at one of the vacant tables with his models of a Packard 8, the company's five-seat sedan, and a Model A Ford sport coupe. Both toys had been sent to him for Christmas by the Anders, a wealthy Jewish family whom his parents had helped leave Germany for the United States in 1936 when they realized Hitler was preparing for war and would carry out his promise of eliminating all European Jews.

The boy looked up and shivered when a tall, stately German officer noisily entered and shouted an order in a language he did not understand.

His father greeted the visitor with a smile and asked, "What can we do for you, Officer."

The man threw back his broad shoulders. Clicking his heels, he said in a loud, guttural tone, "I am SS Obergruppenfuhrer und General der Waffen-SS Heinrich Gropius. Address me always as Obergruppenfuhrer Gropius. I am commander of the Waffen SS (Schutzstaffel) visiting Poland for a short time. While we are here, I expect you to extend to any of my officers your most gracious hospitality. Do you think you can do that?"

"Of course, Herr Obergruppenfuhrer Gropius."

Gropius was taller than Casimir, and without the hint of a smile, he added, "Excellent. You learn fast. We shall work well together. I want you to prepare a meal for my officers who will join you at eight o'clock tonight."

The Nazi officer was dressed in his best uniform with the shiny metals over his left breast.

Casimir asked, "How many should I expect?"

The officer clicked his heels again and replied, "A party of fourteen. You will do this in honor of our führer Adolf Hitler who will be in your city to inspect our troops later today."

Casimir, showing his nervousness, quietly asked, "Shall we expect him to be here?"

"Do not be an ignorant, Dumkoff. He will not, of course."

"Very well, Herr Obergruppenfuhrer Gropius. We shall gladly accommodate the presence of you and your man here at the appointed hour. What would you like on the menu?"

Officer Gropius sat at a table and looked at the menu. He slapped his hand on it and exasperatedly declared, "This is Polish *pfutze*. You understand me?"

Casimir understood that the man called Polish food slop and said to him, "It is what the Polish people want to eat."

"Well, we shall see about that. Here's a list of what I want you to prepare, and if you do a good job, I shall consider you for future parties."

"Parties?"

The officer laughed heartily. "What did you think we were going to do?"

Casimir studied the list: Wiener schnitzel, pork schnitzel.

The officer then said, "Oh yes, make the meals with pork shank and pork knuckle."

Before the officer left, he told Casimir to have plenty of schnapps, good scotch whiskey, and good Kentucky bourbon and then handed the Pole a wad of Polish zlotys.

Casimir immediately went to the market to buy what he wanted and needed for the soldiers' meal. After telling his friend Stanislaus what he was doing, his friend said, "That's treason if you give aid and comfort to our enemies, 'cause those bastards are killing our people who are resisting the invasion and occupation of our free and independent nation."

While Casimir agreed with much of what his friend told him, he said, "I think we have to learn to live with these invaders. If we don't, they will destroy us. Right now, they only want to take over our country and rule it peacefully."

"I can't agree with you, Casimir. Join us. We are planning a fight to take back Warsaw, drive the Germans out, and prevent the Russian Communists from coming here and forming a government."

A month later, Stanislaus was killed resisting the Nazi occupation while fighting as a member of the underground Polish Army.

When Casimir arrived home after shopping, he told his wife, "I think I can exploit the Nazi taste for alcohol, parties, and loose women. I'll pretend to be a friend of the Germans so we can more easily hide Jews, and I'll look for a Catholic soldier who could possibly help me."

Antonina cautioned her husband to be aware of the Gestapo. He told her he would be careful. Two months earlier three Germans had lured many Jews to the Polski Hotel with the promise that the Gestapo would send them to South America, but after Casimir investigated, he issued a warning and saved many Jews from death. Nevertheless, 3,500 Jews went to the meeting and were never seen again.

This Nazi action was part of Hitler's plan to remove all Poles from the country and replace them with Germans, whom he termed racially superior, in order to expand territory for his citizens. He had started with Austria and then occupied the Sudetenland, and by 1939, his forces were occupying Czechoslovakia. Hitler did all of this without arousing armed response from the Allied nations of Britain and France. No country leader wanted to militarily stop him, although Britain and France did declare war on Germany.

The collective Polish people were not going to put up with the German blitzkrieg aggression, and so without waiting for assistance from other nations, they decided to fight. They mobilized one million men even though they knew they would be greatly outnumbered in manpower and armaments with the possible result they could be captured and annihilated.

Casimir and his wife secretly taught the Jews some Catholic prayers and facts of the Catholic religion so they could exist as Catholics in Poland in plain view. He was able to get ID cards for some who were sent to large cities to pose as priests and nuns in a Catholic community; they had to memorize their new Christian names and the history of their new settings and avoid speaking Yiddish, which would have exposed them.

Just before Casimir's first party for Commander Gropius, he took Casimir aside. Smiling, he slyly asked, "You would not mind, would you, if a few of my men took their lady friends up to one of your vacant rooms?" It was not so much a question as a mild order, and this is how Casimir understood it.

He replied to the Nazi officer, "There would be an extra charge for that."

Gropius laughed and said, "Of course. You think we are thieves?"

Casimir didn't answer, because he didn't want to offend his guest, the new authority in the local area.

When his first party was over early the next morning, the general told Casimir, "Let's plan for a party every Friday night. I am sure you could use the income and the protection of my men."

And so a program for such parties was instituted. But it meant that the usual Polish patrons of the inn were angry and said as much to Casimir. "How can you, a Polish patriot, lick the boots of these soldiers who are definitely the devil incarnate and give them priority over your own people?"

And so it was that Casimir was one to avoid, because he was seen as a collaborator with the invaders. But Casimir had a bigger plan in mind— one that would help his fellow Jewish Poles avoid being persecuted and murdered by the Nazis. However, because of Polish anti-Semitism, he would not disclose his plans even to his friends.

Jews Forced into Ghettos

In 1939 the Soviet Union occupied Eastern Poland, according to the terms of the German-Soviet Act of August 1939. Germany annexed most of Western Poland. Part of the partitioned area of Poland was organized into the general government ruled from Kraków by the chief administrator, Gov. Gen. Hans Frank. It was further divided into four districts: Kraków, Warsaw, Radom, and Lublin.

Frank, who was a onetime lawyer for Hitler and the most senior Nazi in Poland, ordered that all Jews in Warsaw and the surrounding areas had to live in ghettos, the specified wall-enclosed areas within Warsaw's boundaries. Thereby, he created a prisonlike area with a population of approximately four hundred thousand citizens, less than 3 percent of the total Warsaw population.

The first Jewish family that Casimir Gorska saved from the ghetto by hiding them from the Gestapo was that of Murray Heisenberg. To make it work, Casimir asked the Borowczak family in his church, Holy Cross on Royal Way, and they agreed to give the family a secret area in their attic.

Usually, a family stayed less than a week before they were transferred to the underground escape system. Many went to Palestine. Casimir sent the Jews to several different locations so as to keep them hidden on the move until they could be taken out of Poland. Before it was sealed in November 1940, many of the Jews from the ghetto in Warsaw came to Casimir for help.

The Jewish Community Council was transformed by the Nazis to form the Judenrat, which represented the wealthy Jews. An orphanage was opened January 31, 1942, on Ogrodowa Street.

Jewish factories produced goods that were smuggled out and sold to the outside residents, the Aryans; products were made from raw materials smuggled into the ghetto. Private firms using Jewish labor within the ghetto also produced products for the German Army.

The ghetto area was enclosed by brick walls topped by barbed wire. The large area of the city was split into two sections fenced on each side of a public street where no Jews were allowed, but non-Jewish pedestrians, cars, and trams freely traveled on the street between the two sections. A bridge over the street connected the two areas, thus providing communication between them without leaving the ghetto. The Warsaw Gestapo was located on Szuch Avenue bordering the ghetto in order to efficiently manage the isolation of the Jews.

Several months after they first met each other, German General Gropius surprised Casimir when he showed up one morning as if he were looking for a place to relax. Casimir motioned for him to join him at a table in a secluded section of the restaurant just outside the door to the kitchen. The Polish businessman said nothing and waited for his guest to indicate what he wanted.

"Some schnapps with a touch of bitters."

Casimir served his guest, sat down at the table, and waited for the general to say why he was visiting when it did not look like a military- based appearance.

Gropius loosened his tie and unbuttoned his shirt as he told Casimir, "We just finished sealing the ghetto, but I am not sure why Hitler hates the Jews so much. Would you have any ideas why he does?"

His host did not know what to think—whether he was being tested or interviewed for a Gestapo report. He didn't answer right away but finally said, "I am sure your führer has his reason for such strategy."

Gropius laughed as he banged his hand on the table. "You don't have to worry, my friend, because I am not here on any official business. I am just trying to get away from the nasty aspects of war." He drank more of his schnapps. "Herr Gorska, is there anything I can do for you?"

It appeared to Casimir that he had made a new friend, but one with whom he would be cautious until his guest proved to be more trustworthy. It was not unusual for Nazis to lure their victims into a net in order to maintain control over them.

About a month later, Casimir witnessed a German soldier shooting a defenseless citizen of Warsaw in the head. This angered him. The victim had a yellow armband with the Star of David, which all Jews were made to wear. And Casimir decided then and there he would work even harder to save as many Jews as possible.

After Casimir gained the confidence of Nazi Gen. Herr Obergruppenfuhrer Gropius, he was able to obtain permission and permits for several Jews in Warsaw to move to Kraków so they could work in Oskar Schindler's factory, which produced products for the German Army. The Jews who worked for Schindler were protected from going to the death camps.

Many of German descent in America, especially those of the Jewish Workers Party (Bund), helped rescue Polish Jewish children. This involved Casimir and his wife gathering the children into small groups for escape.

There was heavy Arab pressure on the UK to keep Jews out of Palestine. Because the UK blockaded Palestine, the Jewish children went through Romania to the Holy Land using smuggling networks called *brikha*. Some went through Czechoslovakia and Hungary to the shores of the Black Sea and then by boat to Haifa through the blockade.

As Casimir's son Jacob grew older, he started smuggling food into the ghetto. Sometimes he would shove bundles through secret openings in the ghetto walls. Other times, in the dark of night, he would throw bundles over the wall into the enclosure. To be caught meant certain death.

His father facilitated false document delivery, such as ID cards, by giving Jews a ghetto laundry claim check with which they could pick up packages containing the forged documents at the laundry.

A month after the ghetto was sealed, groups of occupants were ordered into trucks that were bound for Treblinka, the closest death camp to Warsaw. The travelers were led to believe they were going to a work camp. Very little, if any, true information was available to them, but many in the ghetto suspected that the people taken would never be seen or heard from again. Casimir saved as many of these Jews as possible.

Besides locating Gentiles who took in Jewish boarders for money, Casimir also worked with Bielski family partisans in the forest to rescue Jews by encouraging them to live in the forest. He was distressed that he could not save more Jews. All of this he did in secret, knowing that if he were to be discovered, it meant death.

Sometimes the rescuers found US visas left on Italian liners seized by the British, which were used by the escaping Jews.

Casimir felt confident enough in his relationship with General Gropius that he asked about the transfers from the ghetto. The general told him that he couldn't talk about it but that it distressed him to think that innocent Jews were murdered by execution in the *final solution*, a decision reached by the Nazi leaders during a secret meeting called by Hitler at Wannsee in Germany.

The general told Casimir, "I am a Catholic, and I don't believe that the Jews are the enemy. Our greatest threat comes from Moscow: the Communists. I tell myself this every day in order to live with the horrible aspects of what our nation is promulgating."

Casimir quietly listened and tried to make sense of this man who was pledged to Hitler but did not believe in genocide. He wanted to but did not ask the general why he did not refuse to carry out his orders; he already knew the answer. Several times Casimir would report "bad Jews"—those who revealed the hiding places of Jews trying to escape. It took only one Pole to betray a hundred Jews, but it took ten to save one Jew. Sometimes Casimir would find birth certificates of deceased aristocrats and use them for getting an *arbeitz*, or work card, and a *kennkarte*, or ID card, both of which were foolproof.

Some Jews who were hopeful of returning from the Nazi internment had Gentile friends hold title to their assets to prevent the Germans from stealing them; a few custodians after the war refused to return the assets, and in more than one case, they murdered returning Jews to keep the assets for themselves. The Polish Home

Army was at the forefront of the Polish resistance movement—the largest underground movement in all of Nazi-occupied Europe during the war. It was made up of saboteurs who disrupted German supply lines. They also provided military intelligence to the British.

Toward the end of June 1942, when Gropius made a visit to Casimir's restaurant in the afternoon, he told Casimir of a daring escape from the Auschwitz concentration camp by three Poles led by a Ukrainian. They were all dressed as fully armed, uniformed Nazis and drove an SS staff car through the main gate. They were never captured. The general smiled as he said, "You have to admire the ingenuity."

At the age of seven, Jacob was beginning to understand what was happening to Poland. His father, though, refrained from telling the boy too many details for fear it would scare him. Still, Jacob slowly pieced together the information he gathered by listening to what the German general was telling his father. This is how he learned what was happening in Poland: the explosions, as well as the Jews who were taken from their homes in the middle of the night and then crammed into cattle cars for the trip to the camps.

One day in 1943, while making a food smuggling trip to the ghetto, Jacob noticed that soldiers were leading groups from the ghetto and lining them up for a march to the railway station. That night when he asked his father about what he'd seen, he was told the inmates were being transferred to labor camps. Jacob then asked why the Jews let themselves be placed in the ghetto. After all, there were more Jews than soldiers to guard them.

"Those are the Jews who are afraid to stand up to their captors because they think they will come out alive in the end," Casimir answered.

Then the boy said, "Many of them are killed by the Germans. Why don't they fight?"

On April 19, 1943, Jacob had his answer. Polish Jews began to learn that Treblinka was for extermination and not labor, and they decided they would revolt to avoid that fate. The Polish underground army set up six locations outside the ghetto to fight the Germans. They were greatly unprepared when they fought with whatever few weapons they could obtain and fortified their hideouts to strengthen their fighting power. A plan to breach the ghetto wall with explosives was overcome by the Germans. Some of the resistors' hideouts were the sewers, which Nazis soldiers flooded in order to force them out into the open where they were then shot down. Jewish attempts to defeat the guards and soldiers lasted just four weeks, ending May 16.

Casimir knew that Jewish resistance came only after there was no hope for survival and after faith in the leadership of the Jewish Council that had been created to protect them had been lost. He was able to help the Jewish fighting organization with food, weapons, and ammunition, which he secretly delivered to resistance organizations in the nearby forests. In the end, Casimir knew that the resistance fighters preferred to die killing Germans rather than be carried off like cattle to the extermination camps. He often recited to his friends Luke 22:32: "Christ said to Peter strengthen your brethren."

Nearly one year to the day after Hitler's army was defeated at Stalingrad during his surprise invasion of the USSR, the Soviet Army pushed westward. They liberated the Polish city of Lublin and installed a pro-Communist Polish committee of national liberation in July 1944 that functioned as a provisional government taking orders from Stalin.

General Gropius quietly told Casimir, "On July 29, 1944, the Red Army reached the east side of the Vistula River at Praga, and then they stopped."

Praga was a suburb of Warsaw. Based on prior agreements with Stalin, the Allied powers believed the Soviet Army would cross the Vistula to defeat the Germans and free Warsaw, but Stalin so detested the Poles that he wanted them annihilated and hoped the Germans would do just that.

Gropius added, "This is puzzling. We expected the Red Army to attack us in Warsaw, and we were prepared."

Casimir hesitated and asked the question, "Do you know that we Poles were hoping for the Red Army to drive your army out of Poland?"

The Poles, based on earlier discussions with Stalin's agents, were hoping to get help from the Red Army to push the Germans out of Poland.

"Yes," answered the general. "Soviet Russia is our true enemy, not the people of Poland, but I am a soldier pledged to follow orders. I shall fight for the Fatherland. But also, I do not like many of the führer's orders." He drank the last of the beer from the glass before adding, "I am not a traitor. But I was hoping the death plot against Hitler would have succeeded, because he is ruining my country for his personal glory." The officer then paid Casimir, thanked him for his hospitality, and quietly left the restaurant.

The next and final time Casimir met with General Gropius he told Casimir, "You should immediately take your family to Kraków. The brave fighters defending Warsaw will eventually be conquered."

"But why should I leave Warsaw?" Casimir questioned.

"What I am telling you as a friend who has been good to me and my men is secret information. Hitler has ordered the Wehrmacht to destroy Warsaw so there is nothing left. You won't have any heat or electricity and maybe no water. As a result, your business will be ruined, and you will lose your income, so don't think you will survive. You must take your family to Kraków immediately."

The two men shook hands (unseen by anyone in public) as they said farewell and wished each other a better life, realizing they would never see each other again.

Casimir told his wife and Jacob they would have to move to Kraków and explained what was going to happen to Warsaw. While his wife and son packed their bags, Casimir went to the bank and took out all his money. When he returned home, he, Jacob, and Antonina prayed that they will have enough money and asked God to take care of them until Casimir found gainful employment, bought a restaurant, or started one from the beginning. That same day in the evening, as the sun set, the Gorska family boarded the train for Kraków. Two days later, just as the general had told him, the Germans destroyed Warsaw while the Soviets did nothing.

In order to get settled, the family went to the cathedral and asked Archbishop Sapieha if they could stay just until Casimir found a place to live and a job. The archbishop told them they were welcome and permitted them to live in the diocese castle. The Archbishop had in the castle an underground seminary and in attendance was Karol Wojtyla studying to become a priest; he later became Pope John Paul II.

Casimir took over a failing restaurant. The family remained in Kraków for the duration of the war. After hostilities ceased, he took his family back to Warsaw where he bought an aging restaurant and hotel. After World War II, Casimir created another successful restaurant. The only negative that he saw was that Poland came under the jurisdiction of Stalin—a new tyrant replacing the old.

Book 2

Allies Stabbed in the Back

In February 1945 as World War II in Europe was coming to a close, US President Roosevelt, Britain prime minister Winton Churchill, and Soviet Premier Stalin met on Stalin's home turf in Crimea at Yalta, a city-resort in southern Ukraine on the north coast of the Black Sea, which was a part of the Soviet Union. The work at the Yalta Conference was to thrash out war strategy and agreements that would decide the fate of postwar Europe by a secret plan devised by Stalin to take over Poland after promising at Teheran that Poland would be a free state. Stalin thereby stabbed his three Allied friends—France, Great Britain, and the United States referred as the Big Three—in the back after he used them even as they worked together to defeat Germany.

The Big Three, Allied leaders, eager to meet face-to-face, agreed to Stalin's request for the Yalta Conference. He was in the superior position, because his Red Army troops were a mere forty miles from Berlin. What also placed the Western powers at a disadvantage were Roosevelt's failing health and Britain's increasingly junior position relative to the United States. In addition, FDR thought he needed and could trust the Russians to help defeat the Japanese in the Pacific. The three Allies traded that promised assistance from him for Stalin's requests regarding Eastern Europe, requests that put all of Eastern Europe under the Kremlin's control. On top of that, the Soviets were also granted a sphere of influence in Manchuria following the defeat of Japan.

As for the future of Germany and Eastern Europe, the four Allies decided it would better to divide Europe among themselves to prevent another war. The Eastern portion bordering the Soviet Union was thought to be friendly with the Soviet regime. Stalin pledged free elections in all territories that the four Allies had liberated from Nazi Germany. The French took the Western portion, while the Northern area went to Britain, and the rest in the South to the United States. As for Poland, the trio made the fatal mistake of allowing inclusion of Communists in its postwar national government.

Berlin, Germany, was divided into four sectors controlled by each of the four Allied powers under what was to be only a temporary agreement, dependent upon the sincerity of the Soviet leader.

Stalin, however, as was his intention even as the war was ending, wanted all of Berlin, the divided city that was surrounded by all of East Germany, to be his total domain.

After Roosevelt's death, which led to the presidency of Harry Truman, this attitude was opposed by the other Allied powers, which resulted in a frosty attitude toward the Kremlin. It thereby became the basis of the forty-five-year Cold War between the USSR and the West.

In 1946 Prime Minister Churchill advised the world that there was an invisible Iron Curtain descending around and enclosing Eastern European countries that were allowed to be put under the control of the Soviets by the four Allies at Yalta. In 1952 the Soviets, contrary to agreements made by the Allies, erected a more than four thousand-mile barbed wire fence around Eastern Europe in addition to trenches and barricades.

The Allies financially helped rebuild Europe through the US Marshall Plan. Only Stalin refused the aid. As a result, West Germany recovered and prospered, and West Berlin, with its robust economy, became a thriving section of the divided city.

Jacob Must Go to America

The time was 1949.

That was the year Casimir and Antonina Gorska first discussed sending Jacob to America. They sat at the kitchen table with a neighbor and long-time family friend named Aleksander.

Aleksander looked at his friends with his sad eyes peering out from under the bushy hair that fell halfway down his forehead, almost to his full black eyebrows. He spoke the way most people do who have a sinus problem and nasal congestion.

He said it first. "Jacob must go to America."

Jacob, now fourteen years old, defiantly objected. "I will not leave my home."

Antonina said to her son, "You can bring us there after you settle. A man from Bialystok moved to America and then brought his family from Poland."

"That was nearly ten years ago," reminded her husband. "Now the Soviets control our lives, and it is not so easy."

Aleksander told them, "America is the only country that can help Poland get rid of the Moscow atheists."

"How do you know that?" Casimir asked.

"Word comes to us from the resistance and the Voice of America."

Jacob began sobbing. "I won't leave without Momma."

"In Poland there is a struggle between tyranny and freedom," Aleksander explained. "In America you will be free."

"I will not go to America," Jacob announced before jumping up and leaving the room.

Antonina said, "Our son is scared because he does not understand the situation. It won't be easy going to a strange country and leaving all he knows behind."

Casimir said, "The real problem is that he has no one in America."

Antonina pointed to the picture of the Black Madonna, the mother of Jesus and the patron of Poland. "She will protect him."

Aleksander asked, "Why does she not protect you now?"

Antonina answered, "She does. But in America our son will have a much better future. It is the American way."

"God bless America," prayed Casimir.

Aleksander agreed. "In America anyone can do anything if he works at it."

Antonina turned and pleaded with Aleksander. "Talk with Jacob. Make him understand how limited he will be here and how terrible life will be under the rule of the Moscow Communists. We are old now and can take what happens, but he is young and vulnerable." Antonina began to cry, and Casimir put his arms around her and let her sob.

Aleksander promised, "I will talk with Jacob."

After Aleksander left, Jacob's parents held each other tightly.

Antonina asked, "Will Poland ever be an independent, free, sovereign nation again?"

"We must pray for that to happen," Casimir responded. "The popes have been asking that we pray for the conversion of Russia."

She said, "It will take more than prayers. It will take action."

"We tried in 1944 when we fought for Warsaw to drive the Nazis out of Poland and resist the Soviet takeover," he reminded her. "Stalin failed to keep his promises to help us."

The Soviet leader planned from the start to politically control Poland as a buffer between the USSR and Germany, some of which he finally took control following the Second World War.

Stalin began with the killing of those he felt opposed him or collaborated with the Nazis during the war.

Jacob's parents were on his hit list.

Where Is the Boy?

During the Second World War, intelligence was gathered by many sources and reported to their respective Allied countries. The British Intelligence Agency MI6 cooperated with Soviet intelligence in order to better oppose the Nazis, and some intelligence reached Stalin regarding Casimir Gorska and his relationship with the occupying Germans.

When the Soviet leader saw this information, he immediately catered to his paranoia and ordered the death of Casimir Gorska as an enemy of the USSR because the Pole had a relationship with a Nazi officer, as reported by British intelligence.

One fall evening Casimir and Antonina were startled by loud, forceful knocking at their front door. The couple glanced at each other and then tentatively looked at the door as if they could see who had arrived. Before they could open it, two Soviet NKVD agents rushed inside.

"Where's the boy?" demanded a man with a scarlet mark on his left cheek.

Casimir replied, "He's not here."

"What do you want with him?" asked Antonina, hoping to hide her fear.

"Shut up, woman," the other agent snapped.

The soldier with the scarlet mark said, "I am Lt. Evgeny Biroschnikov of the NKVD. This is my assistant Vladimir."

Biroschnikov stood less than six feet tall. His small blue eyes carefully surveyed the room as he noted specific details that he committed to memory. He surveyed the couple in front of him carefully, noting their body language.

On his command, Vladimir grabbed Casimir. "We have orders to arrest you both."

"Why?" asked Casimir.

Biroschnikov took papers from his coat pocket. "You collaborated with the Nazis during the war, and therefore you have been declared enemies of the state."

Vladimir added, "You supported the 1944 Warsaw Rising to keep the Soviet Union out of Poland."

"Who makes this judgment?" Casimir asked.

"You had your trial, and you were found guilty."

"I was not at any trial. Where was this court?"

"It does not matter. Premier Stalin makes the decision."

Casimir grew indignant and said emphatically, "I did not collaborate with Nazis."

Vladimir shoved Casimir toward the door and hissed, "My parents died at Stalingrad. You—Nazi lover—will pay."

Biroschnikov grabbed Antonina and dragged her from the building.

Jacob, who had been hiding in the cellar under the building, crawled to a window to see what was happening outside.

His mother asked the Soviet agent, "Why do you want Jacob? He has done nothing."

Biroschnikov said, "Comrade Stalin wants all children to get a decent education. He loves children and gives them what they need."

Casimir shouted, "You want to brainwash our son and make him one of Stalin's puppets."

Vladimir hit Casimir in the face with the butt of his rifle. Casimir fought back and kicked the agent's knee. The soldier's leg buckled, causing him to fall.

Casimir said loudly and proudly, "I never collaborated. I pretended to do so only so I could save the lives of my Jewish friends from concentration camps and death. I was never a Nazi."

Biroschnikov shouted, "But you liked the Nazis."

"I was only pretending so I could help my Jewish friends," he insisted.

"You spoke against the Soviet Union."

"The Polish people do not want Soviet occupiers. We must have our independence and freedom just as before the war with Polish rule rather than rule by Stalin."

Biroschnikov told him, "That is treason."

Vladimir rose to his feet, tied the couple's hands behind them, stepped to face them, and held a paper for them to see. Biroschnikov then walked behind Casimir.

Meanwhile, Jacob lay motionless in the cellar without making noise. He clearly saw what was happening, and the more he saw, the more feelings of fear grew within him.

Vladimir officially stood at attention as he read the paper to Jacob's parents. "Casimir and Antonina Gorska, you have been found guilty of treason and are hereby to be executed by the order of our beloved comrade leader, Josef Stalin."

Biroschnikov said, "You are opposed to a Socialist Poland and allegiance to Comrade Stalin. You are enemies of the state." He then placed his gun against the back of Casimir's head.

Casimir, feeling the cold steel of the weapon, said, "You will pay for what you do to the Polish people. You can kill us, but you can't kill freedom."

Biroschnikov pulled the trigger, putting the bullet into the back of Casimir's skull. Antonina screamed and tried to break free. The Russian quickly turned and shot her in the head.

Jacob watched his parents crumble and fall, and he saw the large scarlet color on Biroschnikov's left cheek.

The soldiers laughed as they walked away.

It took some time before Jacob felt enough courage to rush to his parents. Kneeling beside their inert bodies, he cried and screamed in pain. "I will avenge your deaths. I swear I will." But no one was there to hear him.

As the boy grieved, Aleksander slowly approached from the shadows. He muttered, "Christ save us." He checked the couple for any pulse, and when he felt none, he pulled a sobbing Jacob away and held him close.

"There is nothing you can do now."

A crowd of curious people soon gathered.

Aleksander took the traumatized Jacob into the house where he sat the boy down at the kitchen table. Jacob said nothing.

Aleksander told him, "Say something, Jacob."

After a moment, Jacob wiped his eyes. "I could have saved them. I didn't save them." The boy suddenly began to shake violently.

"You are not to blame. How could you save them? The soldiers would have killed you too. It's God's will that you are still alive. He must have a mission for you. God spared you for some reason yet to be disclosed." He put his arms around the youth and hugged him. "Someday the bastards will get what they deserve."

"I will kill them."

"You can't do that," Aleksander told him. "They are strong, and there are too many of them."

"I saw the men who did it," Jacob said.

"You can identify them?"

Jacob nodded. "The one with the red mark on his face shot mother and father. I saw the man. He will come back to take me away or kill me."

"You must stay out of sight until after the funeral. Then we send you away."

Soon, a man named Michael entered the house. He addressed Aleksander. "He must leave here soon—before the Russkies return."

"The boy saw the killers."

"Then we for sure must quickly get him out of Poland."

Jacob attended the funeral mass and burial in disguise. Afterward, Aleksander took him to the home of Aharon Tabory, a Jew whose family Casimir had helped hide from the Nazis.

"Of course I help the boy," he had said to Aleksander.

"But can we get him out of Poland to America?" Aleksander questioned.

Aharon pointed to a picture of the Black Madonna. "She will help us just as she protected me and many others from the Holocaust."

"But the cost. I have no money," replied Aleksander.

Aharon smiled. "Leave that to me. I owe everything to the boy's father. I am sure it can be worked out."

"Who do you know in America?"

"There is a man in Detroit—actually, Hamtramck, the Polish community. Casimir and Antonina also helped him escape. I am certain I can rely on him."

"But—"

Aharon stopped him. "You worry too much. For a Catholic, you have so little faith in your God, Gentile."

Aharon and the boy laughed, but Aleksander sat with a dour facial expression.

Aleksander banged his hand on the table. "All right. Have it your way, but if anything happens to Jacob, I will come looking for you."

Aharon shrugged and winked at the boy. "Jacob, are you willing to do what I say?"

The youth nodded.

"Alek, don't scowl so much," Aharon joked. "It is bad for the digestion."

Alek asked, "Now what are you going to do?"

"Take Jacob to Gdynia, which is close to Gdansk. From there, he takes a second-class passage on a ship to New York City in America."

In order to get Jacob onto the ship, Aharon had to deal with guards at the harbor. He told Jacob, "Let me do the talking. Don't say anything. Our success depends on it."

The frightened boy trembled but remained silent.

They approached the guard.

"Papers, old man."

Aharon handed him a package.

As the guard opened the package, Aharon produced two bottles of expensive vodka and offered them to him.

The guard looked into the package and then glared at Aharon. "You are trying to bribe me, old man."

Aharon calmly answered. "Not at all." He knew the guards could be bribed if they were paid enough money. "I thought you might be cold and lonely. Here is some antifreeze."

Jacob held his breath and looked ahead at a large ocean liner, thinking to himself, *Aleksander for sure is taking us to the firing squad.*

The guard pulled a wad of paper money from the package and quickly stuffed it into his pocket. He then bunched up the paper bag and threw it at Aleksander after taking the bottles of liquor. "You Jews are so stingy. No wonder you have all the money in the world."

Aharon said not a word. He knew the first to blink would lose.

The guard stepped back, spat on the ground in seeming disgust, and waved them through, growling, "And don't try that trick again, old man."

Aharon pulled a medal of the Black Madonna from his pocket and handed it to Jacob. "You must wear this all the time. She will protect you even when you are not in Poland. Once Polish, always Polish. Never forget us after you get to America."

Jacob proudly put the medal around his neck. He kissed the image, smiled, and said, "You're such a good man, Aharon. I want to stay with you."

"Not possible. Things here are going to get worse as the Soviets keep us under their boots and oppress us more. They will try to make all this Russian. It is Stalin's way. You must get a fresh start in the new country." He put money into Jacob's pocket and added, "You will need this until Tadeusz meets you on arrival."

They shook hands, and Jacob asked, "Who is he, Aharon?"

"A man your father helped escape the death camps. He will help you find a new home in America."

They said goodbye, and Aharon sadly watched Jacob walk up the gangplank to enter the ship named *Batory*. Jacob turned and waved before disappearing into the ocean liner's interior.

"I pray you will have a better life," Aharon said to himself.

He watched as the *Batory* slowly disappeared from sight when it moved closer to the horizon.

He's Fleeing From the Communists

Aharon had given Jacob forged documents to get him through Polish customs guards, as well as several pages of notes to show the US immigration officials so he would quickly be processed through Ellis Island in New York. He would be met by a friend, Tadeusz, as arranged by Aharon.

When the boat entered the port at New York, Jacob saw the Statue of Liberty—for the first time, it was not just a photograph. Jacob went to one of the stewards and handed him an envelope with a paper prepared by Aharon. It introduced Jacob and asked if someone on the crew would help him find Tadeusz, a relative who would meet him. A picture of Tadeusz was enclosed.

The inspectors boarded the ship to perform their initial inspection, and when they came to Jacob and saw he had a second-class ticket, one of them said to the other, "I don't think this young boy will be a burden to the public."

Jacob would quickly pass into America as an immigrant who would not be a burden on the country. If a passenger arrived by at least second class, it was assumed he had enough funds to obviate his need for society to take care of him financially.

Next, Jacob underwent a brief health exam and an interrogation, after which he was given his landing slip, which granted him permission to leave the ship and enter New York without going through Ellis Island. One of the crew members was designated to escort Jacob down the gangway to the dock and find the man pictured in the photo. Tadeusz was close by, and he introduced himself to the crew member, who verified it was Tadeusz and let Jacob get his bags and leave.

Tadeusz smoked a large Havana Cuban cigar as he walked Jacob to the customs inspection. When the agent asked Tadeusz if he were had been born in the United States, he showed his Polish citizenship papers. Jacob stared straight ahead. The agent examined the papers and asked, "What about the boy?"

"He is a Polish war refugee."

"Where's his passport?"

"He's fleeing from the Communists. You think they gave him a passport and let him freely leave Poland?"

"Is he seeking asylum?" the agent questioned.

"Yes. All the information is in the paper I gave you for Jacob."

"Okay. Go inside and give the agent behind the counter your name and where we can reach you."

The agent looked at Tadeusz's papers and wrote something on a clipboard. He said, "Take Jacob to the immigration office nearest your point of destination."

"Of course," answered Tadeusz.

And with that, they were waved into America.

"Is everything fine now?" Jacob asked.

"It is. Now let's get on to Michigan."

Where Are We Going?

Tadeusz and Jacob stayed overnight in a comfortable hotel outside New York City. After breakfast the next day, Tadeusz put Jacob's suitcase in the trunk of his Dodge car, and they set off on the two-day journey to Michigan.

Jacob asked, "Where are we going, Uncle Tad?"

"To a family who will take care of you," Tadeusz explained.

"But I thought I was going to live with you."

"That is not possible."

"But you are doing very well."

Tadeusz laughed. "I do all right, but I am much older, and my resources are limited. You will be living with the Ralls family; they have *the* money to give you what you need. You must study, learn, and go to college. You cannot get very far in America without an education. And you must stop talking Polish so much. Talk English as much as you can. You can go further as a member of the Ralls family. But you must study." He looked at the boy. "Promise me."

Jacob answered, "I promise."

They made their trip through Cleveland and Toledo and entered Michigan from the southeast. Tadeusz drove through the city of Detroit to Grosse Pointe.

As Tadeusz's car moved slowly on Lakeshore Drive on the western edge of Lake St. Clair, Jacob quietly yet thoughtfully looked out at the passing scenery—the lake and the large homes surrounded by lush green manicured lawns in front of large estates. Jacob sensed they went on forever.

The boy asked, "Did Father really save your life?"

"Yes. Many of us Jews were sent to the camps with the gas chambers and the crematoriums. Your father hid me, clothed me, and fed me and my family. That's how we survived the Nazis pigs."

"I thought you were father's brother. And a Catholic like us."

"That's what we wanted the Nazis to believe. And it worked."

"Are there many Jews in Grosse Pointe?" asked Jacob.

"Not many." Tadeus paused thoughtfully. "Here we are."

"This Is Inverness, the Rallses' Estate"

Tadeusz drove onto a private road leading away from Lake St. Clair and the village of Grosse Pointe, Michigan. After several minutes, an enormous, sprawling, Tudor-style mansion slowly appeared surrounded by lush, mature, tall trees; acres of manicured lawns; plenty of ornamental plants; and water gushing from Greek-styled fountains that gave the appearance of a cool environment.

The car slowly turned onto the circular gravel driveway, making a crunching sound as it moved around a large, flowing fountain. Tadeusz stopped in front of three wide gray flagstone steps leading to the large front entry area dotted with potted plants and original statuary of Scottish origin that had been imported by the Rallses.

The first person on the estate to see the car approach was Susan, the only child of Malcolm and Martha Ralls. She was comfortably seated on an Italian marble bench in the shady spring coolness of the spacious Inverness garden on that warm, humid day. She was dressed in a white linen blouse and a pleated cotton skirt of light blue that extended midcalf. She wore her auburn-colored hair shoulder length, so it framed her oval face and accented her soft green eyes.

She had been observing with curiosity the men in white coveralls carrying furniture and boxes from the moving truck—bearing the name John F. Ivory—into the house next door. It was the recently completed home of Roger Winslow and his family on land obtained from Malcolm in exchange for a life estate. Winslow called it Fair Grove. He was a prominent and successful Detroit broker and member of the New York Stock Exchange with offices in the tall 1928 historic and stately Penobscot Building situated in the middle of the downtown Detroit financial district. He handled Malcolm's investments.

Watching Susan from behind a bush was Roger's only child, George. Later he would enter her life when he walked across the stone bridge spanning a narrow part of the large hourglass shape of Lake Inverness that Malcolm had installed as a natural barrier between himself and Winslow.

Tadeusz led Jacob by the hand up the stairs and to the heavy, double- wide, thick oak entry doors. Tadeusz pressed the doorbell. Young Jacob listened to the musical chimes coming from inside; the tune was a Scottish air.

The front door slowly opened. A man servant in black tails and tie smiled. "Good afternoon, Mr. Tadeusz," he said.

Jacob stared inside the large foyer area, his mouth opened wide, as he was overwhelmed by the rich surroundings.

Tadeusz said, "Hello, Bert. This is Master Jacob. He will be staying with you."

Bert nodded politely and said, "Welcome to Inverness, young man."

Jacob was too overtaken to say anything.

Tadeusz told Bert, "He knows very little English, but he is happy to be here."

"I can see that. Please come with me. Mr. and Mrs. Ralls and the others are waiting for you in the sunroom."

Jacob tilted his head back as far as he could to look at the ceiling, which was high above the winding staircase leading up from the foyer. It appeared as if it were leading straight to heaven.

Bert asked Tadeusz, "Do you have any bags?"

"Yes. In the car."

"Very well. I'll have Rudy fetch them for you."

Jacob's eyes traced the enormity of the foyer—such a large room. He had never seen anything like it before, and the ceiling seemed to be higher than any building in Warsaw.

Jacob's gaze was suddenly interrupted by a tall man in a business suit walking toward him. He was awestruck and overwhelmed as he looked at the size of the house. The strange man turned out to be

Malcolm Ralls. He scowled, as if Jacob's presence was like refuse dumped on the floor.

Malcolm shouted at Tadeusz, "Remember. I told you not to bring that refugee boy here."

Tadeusz flinched.

Mrs. Ralls called from a faraway room. "Let them in, Malcolm. I said they could come today."

Bert stood in silence, awaiting his cue for what he was to do next.

Malcolm barked at Tadeusz, "Take the boy away. Now."

Tadeusz was turning the boy back toward the front entry and his auto standing on the gravel drive when Martha Ralls appeared behind her husband and cheerfully said, "Mal, let the boy in."

"It's too late. I told them to go away."

Martha did not lose her pleasant expression and told Malcolm, "You are terrible sometimes, dear. Take another Miltown and calm down."

She stepped in front of her husband and rushed to the door.

Then she heard from behind her a loud voice, "I forbid this, Martha."

She called out to the departing guests, "Tad, come back here. Malcolm has changed his mind." She turned to her husband. "It's a good thing the boy doesn't understand much English."

Once Jacob returned to the foyer, Martha knelt and took his hand.

Malcolm, never one to quit even when he knew he was losing, said weakly, "I warn you, Martha."

Mrs. Ralls nudged her husband out of the way and led her visitors across the foyer.

Tadeusz apologetically said, "I don't want to cause trouble, Mrs. Ralls."

"Don't be silly."

Malcolm glared at Jacob. "Take the boy away. We don't want him here."

Jacob flinched at Malcolm's abrasive, booming voice and moved closer to Tadeusz.

"Perhaps now is not the right time, Mrs. Ralls. I call you later."

The boy felt Tadeusz directing him away again as Malcolm boomed, "I forbid what you are doing, Martha—"

"Oh shut up, Mal." She turned to Tadeusz. "How is the boy doing?" There was a warmth in her voice

"He's still in shock. He has withdrawn, and he keeps telling me he will avenge the death of his parents."

"I'll get a doctor to help."

Malcolm's loud voice seemed to vibrate within Jacob. "What are you talking about?"

Tadeusz spoke Polish to Jacob.

Jacob whispered back in Polish. "I don't like Mr. Ralls. Let's go."

Tadeusz nudged Jacob. "Is that what you really want? Then let's go." He looked at Martha Ralls. "Some other time." He then led Jacob away.

She grabbed Tad's arm. "No. I want the boy to live with us."

Malcolm was conquered, and he vanished.

Martha said to Bert, "Have Rudy bring the boy's things up to the west room."

She led the duo down a wide hallway toward a room filled with bright sunshine. Jacob felt better hearing the happy voices of several people talking at once. They were Malcolm and Martha's daughter Susan and her friend Ryan Litchfield.

Malcolm stood and welcomed his guests to Inverness as if he'd never seen Jacob before. He offered the boy his hand. Jacob hesitated to take it at first until Tadeusz nudged him. Malcom continued speaking, while the others were silent. "Meet my family. Our daughter Susan and her friend Miss Litchfield."

Jacob stared at Malcolm, not able to understand what he was saying.

Tadeusz explained, "I'm sorry, but Jacob knows little English. I will translate for you. He began speaking Polish to Jacob, who finally began to smile.

Jacob answered in Polish. "I am very glad to be here. Thank you very much."

Malcolm nodded and motioned Jacob to sit between him and Martha. Susan sat beside her mother, while Ryan lounged in an armchair facing them. Tadeusz sat in a chair next to her.

Ryan Litchfield asked Jacob, "Do you play any sports, Jake?"

Martha Ralls said, "His name is Jacob."

Tad translated for Jacob. "Miss Litchfield wants to know if you play any sports."

Jacob answered in Polish. "Football."

Ryan chuckled. "I understand that. I hope to see you on the pitch soon."

Martha asked, "How was your journey, Jacob?"

Tadeusz translated. "Fine. I never traveled before, but I guess it was a good trip."

Susan said, "We travel all the time. We went to Paris last year. Have you ever been to Paris?"

Tadeusz translated for the blushing Jacob. "No. But I want to go."

The first time Jacob Gorska saw Susan Ralls, he fell in love with her. It was not hard to see. Language was no problem.

Martha Ralls said, "We will have a tutor lined up. By the time Jacob goes to high school in the fall, he'll be proficient in English."

Tadeusz translated for Jacob that he was going to learn English over the summer.

Martha asked, "So, Tad. What are your plans now?"

"Perhaps a fishing trip upstate."

Jacob looked from speaker to speaker, not understanding but hearing the tones in everyone's voice. He looked concerned.

Martha patted his arm. "Do that. Jacob will love it. Call me when you return. I'll have the room ready for the boy."

"Thank you."

"Be back soon, so he can learn English, and in August we'll enroll Jacob at the Jesuit high school."

On their fishing trip Jacob was curious about Malcolm Ralls.

"What is it you want to know?" Tadeusz questioned.

The boy said, "Tell me everything."

Tadeusz gave the young man a short biography:

Malcolm's father was the famous Nathaniel (and Nate) T. Ralls who established his family estate, Inverness, on the western shore of Lake St. Clair in Grosse Pointe, Michigan. He did this when he moved his carriage manufacturing business from New England to take advantage of the new horseless carriage business developing in Detroit. His products had earned their reputation for being every bit as well- built as the Concorde Coach, first made in Concord, New Hampshire, and manufactured by Abbott-Downing coaches modeled after the coronation coach of King George the Third in the nineteenth century.

He had a slogan: "Nothing rolls quite like a Ralls."

Nate's Inverness was to be a secluded verdant world of beautiful affluence, safely distanced from the smoke, noise, and sweat of the auto plants. The Pointe had begun as a popular ideal location for wealthy Detroiters to build their many vacation homes.

At the turn of the twentieth century, Malcolm's father converted his Detroit wagon manufactory to produce bodies for fledgling automakers' companies bearing such names as Packard, Olds, the Dodge brothers, and Henry Ford.

Packard cars were luxury cars, and their market was limited. The Olds motorcar company had eventually been integrated into General Motors to form the Oldsmobile division. The Dodge brothers sold their company to the Chrysler Corporation.

Ford's accounting genius, James Couzens, had tapped into an ever- widening market by continually lowering the price of the car as profits soared.

Nate Ralls had affixed his destiny to GM, which absorbed his company into the Fisher Body Company in exchange for cash and stock.

When Jacob Gorska arrived, Malcolm Ralls had already inherited his father's wealth. The Inverness that young Jacob Gorska was brought to was a one hundred-acre section of slightly rolling hills of rural land overlooking Gaukler Point. It was the same land where

Henry Ford's only son, Edsel died, in 1929 had built his Cotswold-style mansion at 1100 Lake Shore Road on ninety acres and three thousand feet of shoreline. It was, some said, a tribute to what a man could do given the opportunity and having no income taxes to pay.

Young Edsel Ford and Malcolm Ralls became close friends when Malcolm worked at Ford; the relationship lasted until Edsel.

Because his family settled in the Pointe before Ford, Malcolm liked to boast that his family were the first car people to settle there.

Nate, through his association with Couzens, had invested in the Ford Motor Car Company and received a fortune when Henry Ford bought all outstanding shares of the Ford Motor Company held by stockholders other than his family. Edsel had lured Malcolm to join the Ford Company, where he at first worked with Frederick W. Taylor in time and motion studies that perfected Ford's continuously moving production line. Later he worked on Ford's development of the trimotor airplane. During the Second World War, Malcolm oversaw Ford's production of aircraft and engines for the large B-24 bombers at Willow Run, MI.

Jacob and Tadeusz spent two weeks camping and fishing the rivers near Rose City in upstate Michigan. The boy learned how to tie dry and wet flies and deftly handle a fly-fishing pole. They caught enough trout to feed themselves for the trip. Jacob smoked his first Havana cigar given to him by Tadeusz.

"You're getting pretty good at this fishing—for a Polack," Tadeusz joked. "And your English is getting much better."

The night before they were to leave for Inverness, Jacob awoke in a cold sweat. He had dreamed he pursued the man with the scarlet mark on his face and tried to kill him. The man turned and killed Jacob.

The boy jolted upright, frightened and shouting.

Tadeusz rushed into the room and listened to Jacob while he comforted him. "It was only a bad dream. Go back to sleep. You are safe here."

"Are we going back to the Ralls place tomorrow?" Jacob asked.

"Yes. We must get you ready for high school."

What he didn't tell Jacob was that Martha had threatened Malcolm with a divorce if he kept up his nonsense about not letting the young man live with them.

Get an Education in Business

Mrs. Ralls received the results of Jacob's entrance exam from the University of Detroit High School. She called him to the family library. "You did well enough for acceptance. I think you will have to improve your English, and will be you'll have to study a little harder than your classmates."

Because of the distance, Jacob traveled to school in what was called the Grosse Pointe bus. It was driven by a faculty member early enough each day for students to attend Mass before classes. At the end of the school day, he returned by the bus to Inverness. He told Ryan Litchfield that it did not matter to him that some of his classmates who practiced football and other sports after classes thought that he was not a jock.

During the first month of classes, a tall Jesuit studied Jacob walking in the dark brown tiled hallway of University of Detroit High School. He was a scholastic, and his ordination was several years away. Mac, as he was called behind his back by the upperclassmen, stood with his hands on his hips and the sleeves of his cassock pulled back like a fullback ready to charge the goal line. The students were told to call anyone in the cassock Father or Mister.

He spoke to Jacob. "My name is Father McFarland." When Jacob remained silent, he added, "Aren't you going to say anything?"

"Hello, Father."

Father McFarland said, "I've been watching you."

"Why?" Jacob asked.

"What's in your future?"

"A Ford—what else?"

"A smarty, eh?"

"Mr. Ralls said he would get me a job there," Jacob explained.

"You should instead think about becoming a priest and joining the order," the father suggested.

"That's a long way off, isn't it?"

"I could get you into the novitiate right away."

"I don't think I'm ready, Father."

"No? If you refuse the call, you'll end up in some dead-end situation when you reach middle age and regret it."

Jacob spent his weekdays absorbing what his teachers presented. He spent his evenings studying, forty-five minutes for each subject, as his counselors advised. Then he took an hour walk to the lake and back. He spent most of his weekends during the first year studying English with his tutor, Miss Larson, with whom Martha Ralls had arranged to teach him at Inverness.

Two years after he arrived in America, he received his driver's license, and Malcolm bought him a three-year-old Ford Super Deluxe sedan coupe and got him a summer job at Ford's Rouge Plant. He began socializing more with his peers from Grosse Pointe and began dating female students from the local Sacred Heart Convent Catholic School where he went to attend weekly tea dances, which were mixers conducted under strict supervision.

The Ralls family that year spent their two-week annual vacation at their Maine summer home. They were close to the summer home of Edsel Ford's family where his father, the first Henry Ford, had built several family cottages overlooking Seal Harbor, a two-hour drive from Bar Harbor. In 1922 Edsel Ford built his summer estate, Skylands, on Mount Desert Island close to his father's.

Jacob looked romantically upon Henry Ford II's two daughters, Anne and Charlotte. They were both a little older than him and traveled in a high society circle of friends with whom he would never be invited to join. He often felt he was the odd man out in the Grosse

Pointe teen culture of his time. No matter how long he lived in the Pointe, he would never absorb that which the local children had in their blood, so to speak. He felt as if the Grosse Pointe culture was transmitted to the offspring by the parents' genes.

Jacob graduated from high school in the late spring of 1953 with honors. When he walked across the stage to receive his diploma, he felt he should have been happy, but he wasn't because he could not share the moment with his parents. Later in life, he would come to realize that he had cut himself off from friends—from the very people who loved him.

That was also when, for the first time, he began drinking heavily in order to medicate the pain and depression later diagnosed as caused by his feelings of guilt for the failure to stop the murder of his parents.

It was the Rallses' longtime neighbor George Winslow who suggested that Jacob should get an education in business. At the time, they were at one of many graduation parties in the Pointe.

"My dad has a place for you in the firm," George told him. "You can begin working part time in the Detroit office this summer."

Jacob replied, "Ford said I could continue working there."

"You can make more money on Wall Street than beside the River Rouge." George was being groomed to take over his father's stock brokerage business. He added, "After college, I'll see you have a good situation, and later I can offer you a partnership. You and I can conquer the world of high finance."

No sooner had Jacob told him it sounded swell when George asked, "What college accepted you?" George poured Canadian rye whiskey from a small flask into Jacob's glass of punch.

"I am not sure."

George said, "You should apply to Yale. That's where I'm going."

"For sure?"

"For sure. Dad has connections. The Skull and Bones and all that."

"I haven't heard from Notre Dame yet," Jacob noted.

"You want Ivy League, Jacob. Think of your future. The old boy network is how you get ahead—not on your merits."

"Maybe I'll just stay in town and get a degree from U of D."

"No panty raids there, man. Where's the fun?"

George, seeing Father McFarland walking toward them, quickly pocketed his flask and stepped back as he whispered to Jacob. "Don't forget what I said."

George was well aware of the fact that Jesuit high school graduates were prime targets for the order's recruiters.

Father McFarland asked Jacob, "Have you decided?"

"George and I were just discussing which college—"

"I mean, joining the order."

"I don't think I want to be a Jesuit, Father. I want to have a family."

The priest frowned. "The order will be your family."

"I had marriage in mind."

The priest pushed. "Don't turn your back on the Lord, Jacob."

"I've prayed about it, Father."

"Pray some more. I'll be here when you change your mind."

Jacob told him, "After a year in college, we can talk again."

"Go easy on the booze, Jay," Father McFarland said.

Jacob stepped back.

The priest added, "You can run, but you can't hide from the Lord, Son. You'll eventually make the right decision and join the order."

George Winslow waited in the shadows for the cleric to vanish into the crowd of graduates and relatives before he approached Jacob. "Before donning the cassock, come to my bash Friday night. Ryan will be there."

"She's your girl," Jacob responded.

"She likes you."

"I'm not sure, George."

Winslow shrugged. "Yeah, but she can still like you." He winked, laughed, and walked away.

Jacob had not thought about Ryan but at the time he looked forward to checking her out at George's party.

# You Know What to Do, Right?

The garden area of Fairlawn was subtly lit with Chinese lanterns that hung over the spacious lush, green lawn. The air was clean and cool. Jacob tapped his foot and enjoyed the band's jazz music as he looked out over Lake St. Clair. It was Ryan Litchfield's full-length rose-colored chiffon dress with spaghetti straps, low-cut over her tanned breasts, that had Jacob thinking how stunningly attractive she was at four years older than him and a coed at Smith College.

After vanishing for a moment, she suddenly appeared beside Jacob holding two drinks. A cigarette was an accessory to her glossy, red- colored lips.

Jacob smiled. "You're too sophisticated for your own good but exciting to behold."

Ryan was a woman who had an overpowering aura of sex about her. Jacob couldn't get close to her without feeling something arousing inside. It was as if there were a transmitter in her libido that constantly sent out signals he could not help but absorb in his own psyche.

She was of moderate height—a little short of six feet—with a modest, yet attractive full bustline and her hair looked like it was made from strands of gold. Her smile was infectious, and Jacob felt he was easily lost in her hazel eyes.

"What a beautiful thing to say, darling," Ryan told him.

He changed the subject. "The weather is too humid."

"Of course. That's Michigan for you." Ryan reached out. "You should have come to my debutante party, honey."

"I'm sure you looked ravishing."

Ryan took Jacob's arm and directed him toward a rise with a view of the lake where they strolled close to the guesthouse before sitting on a wrought-iron bench. In the distance were the lights of the iron-ore freighters moving slowly in both directions in the darkness. He watched several freighters making their way to the north to pick up iron ore from upper Michigan. The others brought it to the Detroit blast furnaces of industries like the Ford Motor Company.

Inhaling her expensive designer perfume led Jacob to think of Jay Gatsby on Long Island staring across the water at the green light of West Egg where his love interest from the past, the fictional Daisy Buchanan, lived—an alluring imagery created by F. Scott Fitzgerald for his novel *The Great Gatsby*.

In "Have you ever wanted to just get onto one of those boats and go away forever?" Ryan asked.

"Yes. I fantasized about it and even went to the Windsor, Ontario docks, but I got scared and came home."

"Georgie Porgie said you don't have a steady girl."

Jacob said, "That's true."

"Why? You're not queer, are you?"

"Why do you care?"

"You mean about being a queer or not having a steady broad?"

"Both," he answered.

"I don't know. Social instincts, I guess. Why do you disconnect yourself from everyone?"

"Do I really do that?" Jacob questioned.

"Don't be angry with me, lover. Some in our crowd think you're avoiding us pointers."

"That's bullshit."

"Well you don't have to be so fucking defensive about it, darling." She lit a cigarette. "I'm thirsty. Want another?"

"Sure."

They went to the bar together, and Ryan reached over and gently stroked Jacob's cheek. "You want to ask me out?"

"George would kill me."

She laughed. "It's true that he fucks me now and then, but he doesn't own me."

"So you want me to ask you out on a date?"

"Sure," she told him. "I think it would be fun. Let's go to Walled Lake for a weekend. I'll get a room and celebrate your graduation."

"Let's dance and discuss it." He drank his highball and pulled her toward the dance floor, although he was slightly tipsy.

George Winslow was chatting with a close friend nearby and chuckled when he spotted him. Without a care, he said, "There she goes. She will seduce him."

"How can you be so sure?" the friend questioned.

"Because," George answered, "I set it up with Ryan."

When the music stopped, Ryan asked, "You really going to work for Georgie?"

"He sure talks a lot," Jacob noted.

"Well?"

He answered, "I told him I could try it this summer and see how I like it."

"Where are you going to college?"

"Wherever will have me."

She told him, "You have a small opinion of yourself. Any college admissions officer would die to have you."

"Is it true stockbrokers can make a lot money?" Jacob asked her.

"If you work hard enough—like anything. George's old man has done very well peddling Wall Street paper."

"Did Joe Kennedy fleece investors?"

"And also bootlegged his way into wealth and power," Ryan noted.

Jacob said, "I won't do anything if I have to be dishonest to get rich."

"Very noble, darling." She looked over his shoulder at George and winked.

George gave her the high sign and turned away toward Buffy Richardson, one of the many young women falling out of the top of her dress.

"Well, you don't have to make wealth your goal, darling," Ryan pointed out.

"What other goals do you suggest?"

Ryan was not shy about telling him. "Sport fucking would be fun, and I'm a fun girl." She then led a surprised Jacob from the dance floor into the house, across the foyer, to the spiral staircase, and down a hallway. "There's something I want to discuss with you." She opened a door.

He asked, "Whose room is this?"

"It's ours now, darling." She closed the door and leaned against it while enjoying the image of Jacob standing awkwardly in the center of the room.

He told her, "You should know I haven't done this before."

She locked the door. "So what else is new?" She slipped out of her pumps, unzipped her dress, and let it fall to the floor.

His gasp was a bomb exploding. His eyes traced the curves of her slender, tanned nakedness. Jacob's breathing became heavier, faster. She slowly walked to him, placed her hand on the front of his pants, and gently felt the budding bulge.

She breathed into his ear. "Let's get horizontal, darling."

"I know what you want, but I didn't bring anything."

"When you're naked, I'll put a rubber on for you." She stepped back and jokingly asked, "You know what to do, right?"

"I guess so. It's nature, right?"

She laughed. "Let me play teacher, and you be the good honors student, lover," she advised as she placed his hands on her bare breasts and began undressing him.

Jacob flinched. "I'm not sure about this, Ry. It's wrong."

"Only if you've been too long with the Jesuits. You won't go to hell. I assure you."

After she removed his shirt, he put his arms around her and pulled her close.

She pushed him down into the cushy bed and bent over so her hot, full breasts dangled over his face and then rubbed them against his body. She breathed into his ear. "I'm not done. Relax." She pulled his pants down over his ankles where she let them fall to the floor as she looked up at the overfull front of his shorts. She advised, "Don't get too ready too fast, darling."

His full member sprung up loose when she pulled his briefs down. As she unrolled the Trojan condom on his turgid organ, she told him, "We want to make the moment last."

She pulled herself on top and slowly inserted him inside her well-lubricated entry point. Rapidly breathing into his ear, she sighed, "God. Your cock is like a rock."

She rapidly thrust her pelvis hard against his and breathed. "Don't tell me you don't like it."

Before he could respond, he was moving rapidly inside her. He couldn't get enough and wanted the action to last forever. He exploded with a cry of joyous pain.

When they were finished, she said, "That didn't last long, but then again, it is your first time." She lit a cigarette and lounged beside him.

He didn't know exactly how long it was before she was asleep in his arms, breathing quietly, and he soon followed.

I Think We Both Need to Take a Break

George, Ryan, Susan, and Jacob waited outside the University of Michigan ice hockey team's dressing room. They were waiting for Ted Fontaine, a star forward on the first line who helped the Wolverines defeat their rival, the University of Denver, which advanced them to the playoffs.

Susan asked Jacob, "Is it true you're going to work for George and his father?"

"Yup, and he is making me a good offer."

"Doing what exactly?"

"Selling stocks and bonds."

A tall player emerged from the dressing room, and Ryan walked up to Ted. "I want you to meet my friends." She pulled Ted by the hand. "Meet Susan Ralls. She's your biggest fan. And Jacob Gorska—, he's my biggest fan. This is Ted Fontaine, U of M's Rocket Richard."

Susan reached out and lovingly took Ted's hand.

George stepped forward and shook his hand. "If you ever want investment advice, call me first."

Ted said, "Let's get some pizza, gang. I am starved."

The group walked a short distance to an Italian restaurant. Dance music greeted them, and after they took a table, Ted told Jacob, "Life is not bad for a Polish refugee, eh?"

Jacob laughed. "Just a guest passing through, buddy."

Ryan said, "Jacob and I plan to stay in Grosse Pointe, though. Don't we, darling?"

Susan said, "But I thought Jacob was off to Italy in the spring to study history."

Ryan looked surprised. "I didn't know that. Why didn't you tell me, darling?"

"I thought I did."

Silence settled over the group until Ryan spoke up. "We'll have to talk about that later. I don't know if I can get away."

Ted laughed. "Rich folks with their heavy decisions."

Susan said, "Dance with me, Ted."

As Ted and Susan went to the dance floor, Ryan pulled on Jacob's arm. "Let's join them, darling."

"I need to talk with you, Ry."

"If you want privacy, we can sit in the cocktail lounge."

Jacob waited for Ryan to sit down.

She asked him, "What's wrong, darling?"

"I think we need to take a break."

"Is that why you planned to go to Italy without me?"

"No. It's a study abroad program," he explained.

Ryan stood, showing not a little anger. "I wondered when you were going to dump me for another broad."

"Don't take it that way. There is no one else. I think we really have nothing going for us except the sex."

"What?"

"It's not that I don't love you, but there is no intimacy between us. Just good sex."

"That's what sex is," Ryan noted. "Sex."

"I want intimacy, something deep between us—not just being physical together."

"What bullshit, man."

"I mean, we don't have any goals in life—just partying and working."

"That's life, darling. What do you expect? Fireworks and music?"

"Some meaning in my life," Jacob told her. "Something that amounts to something."

"Listen to yourself. Why don't you become a priest? Or become president of the United States?"

"At times, you're so insensitive to my feelings, Ry. How can we ever have a solid relationship?"

"And you think selling stocks will give meaning to your life?" Ryan asked.

"No," he admitted. "That's why I'm going to Italy to sort out things."

"To find yourself, right?"

"Something like that."

"Well, you just go to Italy. When you and your sorted-out self get back, I might not be here for you. Go and sort that out."

Jacob excused himself. Ryan sat alone in the middle of the cocktail lounge fuming with anger, silently watching him exit the room.

It took a month before Ted Fontaine fell in love with Susan. It was just before he was ordered to go to US Air Force pilot training. After he got his wings, Ryan and Susan threw a party for him at Inverness.

Susan asked Ted, "So where are you going?"

"Korea," he told her.

At the end of the spring semester, Jacob told Malcolm and Martha that he wanted to travel in Western Europe for the summer to study history abroad.

Ryan asked, "Has Mickey the Jebbie recruiter been on your ass again?"

"It's not that," Jacob told her. "I've never been to free Western Europe. Others I know are doing it."

"I was there two years ago. I guess you should go and broaden yourself."

"You'll miss me, right?"

"Hell no," she told him.

He said, "I'm going to miss you."

"Like hell you will. You'll find some war refugee parasite wanting to get to America by using her charms."

"Don't talk that way, please."

"Okay. Run away. Hide from life. See if I care. See if anyone really cares."

"I'm not running away. What's so bad about wanting to see what remains of the Western world?"

She smiled. "Nothing. Look what it got Columbus."

"I'll study European history in Italy," Jacob reminded her.

"Or find some Greek guy who'll take it in the ass."

"Say. Why don't we go together since you're so upset about me going alone?"

"I'm not upset. I have to complete my studies at Smith. I might get a job in Paris later. Besides, going with you would be a drag. I'd want to get laid, and you'd want to study."

"Is sex that important for you?" Jacob questioned.

"Freud says it makes the world go around," she noted.

"Not money?"

"I want both, lover," Ryan told him.

The next day Jacob started getting ready for his trip to Italy.

Commies Are Everywhere

Jacob walked down the winding stairs of Inverness to confer with Malcolm and Martha Ralls about his plans for summer in Europe. When he heard Malcolm's loud, booming voice bouncing off the walls, he stopped.

"The dirty bastards want to strike," Malcolm thundered.

"Please, dear, I'm right here," said Martha.

"The goddam union says if they don't get a goddam 10 percent wage increase, they'll strike."

Susan walked into the study. Her father turned. "How's my little princess?"

"Fine. George Winslow is here," she said.

Malcolm turned toward the guest. "I hope my daughter has been properly entertaining you, Son." He shook the young man's hand.

Martha told Malcolm, "Chick Chickering wants you to crew on his yacht over the weekend."

"I may have to go to Washington, Martha. It's the damn mess that Henry the Deuce created at Ford—what happens when a boy tries to do a man's job."

Susan's father felt he had to explain. "The boy Ford halted production and laid off sixty thousand workers, and he wants to get all the motor company leaders in a room so they can convince the unions to help with the labor cost problems."

Martha added, "And I suppose Walter Reuther, young and fiery, wants to look good to the United Auto Workers rank and file by bringing the auto companies to their knees."

George announced, "My dad says Communists run all the unions."

Malcolm rose to the bait. "Good thinking. Commies are everywhere, Son."

Jacob noticed as he entered the room how George looked very pleased with himself for contributing something to a man-level conversation.

After Susan left with George, Jacob told Malcolm and Martha he wanted to visit and study in Europe for his junior year.

Mrs. Ralls said, "I think that's a wonderful idea. Will you be going to Poland?"

Jacob answered, "No, ma'am. If I did, I might never return."

Malcolm laughed. "Aren't you glad now you fled that country?"

"When will you leave?" asked Mrs. Ralls.

Jacob answered, "in two weeks."

Malcolm told him, "tomorrow we'll go to the bank for air travelers checks."

I Never Promised You That

Jacob flew to Rome, and before the end of his first month, he was already having Italian lady troubles. They came to a head while they were seated at an outdoor café table on the Piazza della Signoria in Florence. It was just minutes after they had toured Palazzo Pitti and Museum.

"What do you mean we aren't getting married?" Tina of Lucca shouted.

He finished his glass of Chianti before he responded to her. "Did I ever ask you to marry me?" he asked.

"I thought it was understood." She stood.

"By whom?" He asked.

"My family."

"I hardly know you."

She shouted, "But you spend time in bed with me." She stood, gave him the Mussolini pose with her jutting chin, and shot him a glare that would knock over a military squad.

"Please, sit down," Jacob said gently. "You're creating a scene."

She leaned across the table and got in his face. "What kind of woman do you think I am?"

"You're a good woman but not someone I want to marry."

"You can fuck me, but you can't marry me? You promised to take me to America."

"I never promised you that. It's what you expected," Jacob pointed out. "Besides, it would never work out."

She sat down close to him, gently massaging the inside of his thigh. "We can make it work, *caro mio. Te amo.* I love you."

He spoke softly. "We had our fun, and now I'm moving on."

She slapped his face and abruptly stood up, nearly knocking the table over. Her glass, partially full of wine, toppled and broke. Jacob nearly stopped all of the red fluid from soaking the crotch of his light- colored Armani trousers.

"*Bastardo maximo*. Fuck yourself." She swung her hand to hit him again, but he caught her arm. "Well, *Jacobaby*, I don't need you. I have plenty of men who will marry me."

"I'm sure you do."

"I will go back to my true lover, Armando. He waits for me."

"Is he your pimp?" Jacob asked with a chuckle.

"He can whip your puny ass any day." Okay

The Morning Train to Yugoslavia

Jacob took the morning train from Italy south to Pula in Croatia, Yugoslavia. The Hotel Brioni was located on the beach in the northern section of the sunny Istria coast, the Yugoslavia Riviera south of Trieste, Italy. It had seen better days, as evidenced by the peeling exterior gray paint. But it still had a stately structure of serious architecture with its pronounced Victorian-era features, such as balconies and dormer windows on the roof. Room windows were narrow, tall, and seriously reflecting a bygone era of affluence found in that time in history.

He had found entering the Communist country easy. In a letter to Ryan, he wrote: *"The Marshall Tito government is not under the oppressive influence of Moscow. Tito wants to avoid all Kremlin influences that might disturb his personal brand of Communism."*

Jacob was in the crowded dining room of the Brioni having lunch at a table overlooking the Mediterranean Sea. The artwork of the building seemed to Jacob to be influenced by medieval designs. The beach below was clean and bright. Certain areas of it were occupied by topless and nude bathers.

A young, attractive woman in her twenties entered the dining room, looked around, and saw that all the tables were taken. Jacob caught her eye and motioned for her to join him.

Her tall, slender body was well shaped, like an athlete's, and she walked gracefully, like a panther. Her short, dark hair symmetrically framed her narrow, ivory-toned face punctuated by dark eyes and well-formed lips. Her straight nose was centered in her face, making it symmetrical, especially complemented by her high cheekbones.

As he stood, he said, "My name is Jacob. Please join me?"

She said hesitantly, "I am Karyn. Thank you."

He helped her into a chair.

"Are you American?" she asked.

"Yes."

"Do you live here?"

"No. I'm taking a trip from my studies in Florence to explore the ancient history in this part of Europe."

"So you are on vacation. How nice."

"If I were, I'd have picked a better hotel."

She answered, "This place is all about the location. The beach behind the hotel is worth the stay. You don't come here for the accommodations. You're here for the beach."

"I guess that is a good Marxist explanation that would please Tito, but I find the beach unimpressive and inferior to others I have visited," Jacob noted.

"I don't understand your attitude," she said as she studied the menu. "You might then want to try the beaches at Dubrovnik, which I understand are quite nice."

"Your English is good," Jacob told her. "Where did you learn it?"

"My mother taught me."

"And you are here for what reason?"

"I am a member of the ice skating company performing at the arena," Karyn explained.

"I saw the poster. Is it a good show?"

She laughed brightly. "The best, except for me."

Jacob motioned for a waiter. "You'd better order before the kitchen closes."

"Just a salad, please," she told the waiter. "And espresso." Jacob asked, "Where are you from?"

"East Berlin."

"I'm sorry."

"For what?"

"Aren't the Soviets nasty occupiers of your country?"

She laughed. "Not really. We have our own government. There are rules we must follow, but it's like the West. I'm sure you have rules in America too."

"Yes, but your country is surrounded by an iron curtain. You live in a prison."

She answered, "I really don't see it that way."

"Can you leave your country?"

"We can travel. Some of us work in West Berlin and live in East Berlin because West German marks go further than East German ostmarks."

He said, "But aren't some of your relatives living in two different cultures? The East and the West?"

"We visit each other. As long as we follow certain rules, nobody cares."

Karyn's salad arrived quickly.

"I wouldn't be too sure about things, Karyn. You should get out from under the Soviet domination."

"Don't be so dramatic. We do very well, thank you."

"You aren't free, Karyn," Jacob pointed out.

"Yes we are." She smiled and ate her salad.

Jacob told her, "I want to see you again."

"But it is impossible."

"No it's not. I'll contact you."

She set her fork next to the empty salad plate. She stood and said, "Goodbye, Polish Jacob (*Yakub*). It was very nice meeting you."

That evening Jacob took his seat in the arena thirty minutes before the ice show performance began. He looked around the large building that was cold due to the large area of ice that had to be kept frozen. He watched Karyn doing figure eights during the warm-up for the performers.

The show began with music. Jacob felt his body relaxing as his eyes followed an ensemble of skaters dressed in colorful Yugoslavian costumes of the past. They entertained the audience with their precision skating. The original skaters left the rink, the lights dimmed, and when the next group was in their places, the arena suddenly filled with brightness.

Several skaters came onto the ice, and Karyn soon appeared. Jacob looked intently at her as she skated to the music of Don Juan Opus 28; it was gay, light, and rhythmical. He loved watching her glide gracefully over the ice, performing her perfect jumps and spins with confidence and ease.

He said to a woman seated beside him, "She's good enough for the Olympics. Wouldn't you agree?"

The woman didn't understand his English, but out of courtesy, she nodded as if in agreement.

After the show, Jacob waited outside the skaters' dressing rooms. He paced back and forth, furtively glancing at the women's door each time it opened, but always someone other than Karyn came into the corridor. It was an old building that needed paint on the walls. The hallway was soon crowed as skaters came from the dressing room. His anticipation grew with each passing minute.

When Karyn finally emerged, she looked surprised. "You again. Why do you follow me?"

"I liked your skating," Jacob told her.

"Thank you."

Jacob thought she didn't really want to leave, and they visited in the corridor until she told him, "I'd better not be caught talking to you."

"What are you afraid of?" he questioned.

She answered, "You are from the West, and we have been taught to avoid you."

"I don't understand. Why would you be told that?"

"I have no information for you. Don't follow me."

Jacob did not allow her sternness to interfere. He persisted. "I thought we could be friends."

"You're probably the CIA spying on me."

"I am not." Then he suggested, "Let's get something to eat."

"I can't. We have a curfew."

"Tomorrow for lunch?"

"I can't."

The next day when Jacob entered the dining room for lunch, he found Karyn seated at the table they had occupied the day before. He joined her. She did not resist.

He told her, "I was afraid I wouldn't see you again."

When the waiter arrived, the pair ordered their meals. He asked for a ham and cheese sandwich, and she ordered a plate of pasta with Alfredo sauce.

After a short time of silence, during which each studied the other, he asked, "Why were you rude to me last night?"

"I was being watched," she admitted.

"You skated beautifully. Will you be in the Olympics?" he asked her.

"I hope so."

"I'm going swimming this afternoon. Come with me."

"I can't."

Jacob asked, "You can't swim?"

She laughed. "I know how to swim, but I shouldn't be seen with foreigners like you."

"I'm not a foreigner. I was born in Poland."

She said, "But you are American, right?"

"Yes, and you told me the other day that you were free and that you don't have to worry."

"I also said there are certain rules."

He told her, "You should get away from the Soviets. Do you know what they can do to you?"

"My mother won't leave. I am all she has."

"I thought the Marxist concept was that she would have the entire country as her family."

"You are mocking me," Karyn said with a scowl.

He came back, "You are an adult. You can do what you want."

She startled Jacob when she said, "I must not see you again. I am told you will fill my head with the wrong ideas."

"What ideas?"

"About the decadent West."

"Of course. You were told Americans are bad people?" He smiled. "I thought you were going to say ideas about sex."

She told him, "Sex is not a crime."

"Well, then we should make love and not talk about the decadent West."

"You really are a strange person." She laughed. "I don't know why, but I like you. America wants to invade our country because we have so much more than you do."

"You have more totalitarianism, that's for sure."

"I don't understand."

Jacob explained, "We have freedoms in the West that the Soviet Bloc countries do not permit."

Karyn looked sideways at a woman standing near the door watching her.

"My observer is here. I must go. I am probably already in trouble." She stood. "Goodbye, Polish Jacob. It was very nice meeting you."

Jacob told her, "I want to see you again."

"So do I, but it is impossible."

"No it's not. I'll contact you," he promised.

After his swim and a light dinner, as Jacob walked alone to his hotel room, two men noiselessly approached in the dim light cast by the small wall-mounted lamps. Jacob strolled leisurely in the delightfully cool evening air. He wasn't aware of them until they pinned him against the exterior wall of the building where his room was located.

"We don't like Americans," said the first thug.

Jacob told him, "Then don't move to America."

Thug number two hit Jacob in the gut. As he doubled over, he heard, "He means you don't ever see Karyn again. You unnerstan?"

As he caught his wind, Jacob said, "Your English is quite good. Where did you learn it?"

"We watch lotsa Hollywood movies. I like James Cagney, tough guy." He slapped Jacob's face. "Yeah, wise guy."

The other thug pushed Jacob hard against the wall; his head snapped back from the hard surface. He felt a headache begin.

"We listened to *Dragnet*."

Next, the thug punched Jacob in the kidney area, and he dropped to his knees in pain. His attackers walked away, laughing and chatting.

In the hotel restaurant the following morning, Jacob sat at a table drinking coffee and studying the beach activity. Karyn entered the room and walked to his table.

"What happened to your face?" she asked.

He had difficulty breathing as he said, "Good morning, sweetheart. Two thugs paid me a visit last night as I was walking to my hotel room."

"Did they rob you?"

"No. They just wanted to tell me not to see you again."

Karyn laid her hand on his. "I am sorry. I was afraid this might happen, and I warned you."

"So what are you doing here? You said we would not meet again."

"I know I said that. Are you angry with me?"

"No, but I am concerned you'll get into trouble using all that freedom you have."

"I have been thinking about our conversations. I don't care."

"Will your minders who attacked me make your life miserable?" Jacob asked her.

"No," she assured him. "Those weren't my minders, but I think I know who did this to you. Two boys in the troupe want to love me, but I can't stand them."

"Isn't love grand? Jealous lovers."

Karyn stood and answered, "Yes. I have to go now. I'll come to your room after tonight's show. Please be there."

That evening there was a gentle, timid knock on his door. Jacob set aside the text on ancient Rome that he was studying. Karyn rushed through the door into his arms. They tightly hugged. He kissed her lips, stroked her back as he moved farther into his room, and closed the door with his foot. He breathed in the sweet scent of her freshly shampooed hair. They held their embrace a long, loving time. She didn't take her lips from his but pulled him tighter against her warm body. Jacob pulled her with him as he walked backward toward the bed. He pulled Karyn on top of him.

She said, "We shouldn't be doing this."

"I know. It's terrible." He began to unbutton her blouse. "Is this your first time?"

She gently pushed his hands away. "No, honey. We must talk first." She removed her blouse but left her bra in place.

He said, "Can't we talk later, darling?"

Karyn stood and paced around the room.

He looked at her well-rounded breasts and well-curved legs when he asked, "What is it?"

"After tonight, you'll be gone."

"We should make the best of it."

"What if I really like you?" she questioned. "Then what?"

He thought he had the answer. "Come to Italy with me. We can leave right away."

"Do you have a car?"

"No. I came by train."

"Damn. That won't work. I could hide in a car. The border here is not as well guarded as East Germany."

He promised, "I'll order a car as soon as the desk opens."

"Oh, darling." She moved closer to him. "On second thought, it won't work."

"Why not?"

"I would never leave my mother."

Jacob put his arms around her. "Would she come with us?"

Karyn stepped back. "She would never leave her friends and relatives. She was asked before to leave East Berlin, and she refused."

He moved closer to her. "Let's just have each other for tonight. I could visit you in Berlin."

She kissed him many times as they frantically made themselves naked. They took their time. Jacob moved slowly. When he touched her sensitive areas, she made sounds of deep satisfaction.

"I have never been loved like this before," she told him. "It's wonderful here with you."

Jacob looked into her eyes. "More than anything, I want you to come to America with me."

He let Karyn move on top of him. She stared into his eyes as she felt him entering her. She sighed deeply, making sounds of pleasure as she moved against him. Jacob began to thrust heavily against her body, feeling her increasing arousal causing him to feel closer to climax himself.

Suddenly, she began to shutter and cry out, her body tensing and then collapsing against him just as he felt himself finishing.

After a few minutes, Karyn lay on her back beside him and felt her breathing returning to normal. They both said nothing until she spoke.

"If I go with you, my mother will feel that I abandoned her."

"I could come to Berlin and drive both of you to the West."

"How would you do that?" she asked.

"I'll figure something out that will work."

Karyn told him, "I'll try to persuade mother to leave."

"I'll help you obtain exit visas."

"That might work."

Jacob stroked her hair and caressed her cheek. "I'll figure a way. I can work through the state department. There must be some way."

Karyn nestled against him. "I hope so, darling," she said before falling asleep.

They were startled awake to see a man and woman standing beside their bed.

Karyn's face showed fear. "They've found me. I have to go."

The strangers remained menacingly silent.

Jacob asked Karyn, "How much trouble are you in?"

"I'm not sure," she admitted.

The woman told her companion to leave the room and ordered Karyn to get dressed. "*Mach schnell*," the woman shouted.

Karyn kissed Jacob, grabbed her clothes, and quickly dressed.

Jacob silently stared at the woman. He mentally compared her ample figure to a Russian T-34 Tank.

The woman grabbed Karyn and roughly pulled her from of the room as the man reentered the room, knocked Jacob down, and kicked his ribs. He said, "You Americans never learn a lesson. You're lucky I don't kill you, bastard. Should have stayed in Poland."

They Just Love to Harass Americans

At the end of the week, Jacob first saw Karyn's group leave for Germany and then finished his historical research in Trieste before going to Rome where he boarded a night train Wagonlit Pullman car to Florence. After breakfast at the Trinity Bar, he went into the American Consulate to start the process for Karyn's exit visa to visit the United States. He then had to return to Rome to complete his application at the American Embassy before flying Alitalia to Detroit, Michigan.

By 1960 about two and a half million Germans residing in the Soviet sector of Berlin had fled to the West, including the best and brightest of the DDR (German Democratic Republic). To stop this bleeding of its humanity, the Soviets and East Germans ordered a wall built to trap all East Berliners in a quasi concentration camp.

This is what Jacob and Karyn witnessed that early Sunday morning of August 13, 1961. It happened at one o'clock in the morning while they were asleep in Karyn's cozy bed.

"What's that?" exclaimed Karyn, suddenly sitting upright. She awakened Jacob.

Still sleepy, he asked, "What do you want?"

"Listen. What's that noise and commotion going on outside?"

They went to the window and looked down at the street below. Armed soldiers stood guard to prevent pedestrians from crossing the line they had set up in the area where workers dug holes in the ground. They appeared to be installing concrete posts and stretching barbed wire in between.

Karyn said, "What are they doing?"

He answered, "What was feared. Your government is shutting the last remaining revolving door between East and West."

"I guess you were right. I have to get to the West before it's too late."

Jacob held her close when he said, "I'm afraid it's already too late. The soldiers and police are stopping anyone from crossing."

"What about you?" Karyn asked.

"I may be trapped here," Jacob admitted.

She said, "That's not possible. Is it?"

"Looks like it is, but I might be able to cross the line because I have an American passport."

The couple dressed, and before breakfast, they went down to get a better view of what was happening at the center of Berlin. The crowd was growing larger and noisier as protesters shouted objections to workers installing the barriers. The soldiers formed a human chain, holding their rifles at the ready. Motionless, expressionless, they watched the people pressing toward them. If people stepped too close, they were forced back with rifle butts and the hands of the police and militia pushing against their bodies.

After talking with one of the guards, Karyn told Jacob, "I don't understand. The border is sealed. We are trapped."

He told Karyn, "That barbed wire is meant to keep citizens from fleeing to the West. I'm not a citizen here. Why would they want to keep me?"

Karyn said, "What are you going to do?"

Jacob didn't know what to do. Perhaps he could return to the West and persuade the United States and continue to get Karyn and her mother exit visas to leave East Germany for the West.

That evening the secret police knocked on Karyn's door. When she opened it, they barged in. The lead police officer checked documents and then told Jacob, "You must leave East Berlin."

"Why?" asked Jacob. "I am doing nothing wrong."

"You are subverting a citizen of the greatest nation in the world."

"That's just so much bullshit," Jacob told him.

"Do you have a visa to enter East Berlin?" the guard asked.

"No," Jacob told him. "I didn't need one to enter."

"Well, now you do. You are here illegally, and we could arrest you now."

"What's going on?" he asked.

The police told him, "If you are not gone by midnight, you will be arrested."

Jacob studied his adversaries and realized they meant business. He knew what the Soviet-led East Germans were capable of; his dead parents attested to that.

"I'll be gone by midnight," he assured the officers.

The officer said, "If you want, go to West Berlin where you can apply for a visitor's permit."

After they were alone, Jacob turned to Karyn. "I don't know what else I can do. If I stay, they'll arrest you too. If I go, they should leave you alone. I don't think they want to hurt you."

Jacob reluctantly returned to West Berlin even though Karyn had protested. "You're an American. American soldiers occupy part of this city," she told him. "They can't just order you about. Stand up to them." He told her that he did not want to get her in trouble. Before he kissed her goodbye, he promised he would get the visas for her and her mother. "I'll work through diplomatic channels."

She held him close and said, "Call me when you get across and tell me everything is okay."

When Jacob tried to leave the Berlin Russian sector, he was stopped by the police and escorted to a small building on the eastern side of the fence that was under construction. Officials made him wait, and several guards glared at him. The room was small, and the air was hot and smelled bad. After an hour, he was shown to a desk where the official asked to see his passport.

As Jacob showed his document across the desk, the border guard in the uniform said with a scowl, "You work for the CIA."

"Of course not," Jacob answered.

The stone-faced official stared menacingly at him. "How would you like to spend ten years in our prison?"

"I don't think I would like that."

"If you tell me who you really work for, the judge will be lenient with you. We don't like American spies."

"Let me call the American Embassy," Jacob said.

"I am afraid that is not possible. You have entered the country illegally, and you must stand trial."

After being held an hour for interrogation, Karyn walked into the room accompanied by a man dressed professionally in a suit and tie. He shook hands with Jacob and said, "I represent the American Ambassador in West Berlin. Gather up your things. You are free to leave, and I will escort you into the American sector of Berlin."

The East German official behind the desk said nothing. After Jacob and Karyn hugged, kissed, and said goodbye, the embassy agent and Jacob passed into West Berlin. He told Jacob that the border officials had no grounds for detaining and interrogating him.

"They just love to harass Americans," he noted.

Was It Good for You?

Jacob's attempts to get Karyn and her mother visas were discouraging. As a result, he slowly faded back into his former life. He told himself that the love affair was a folly of his youth, a passion of the flesh at a moment of weakness. And he went into a mental depression. He did not want to eat, he did not want to do anything. He he told Martha Ralls that he felt his life was at an end.

A psychologist recommended by Martha told him, "Your condition is due to your guilt and sadness over Karyn. You will have to deal with these."

A month after returning to Inverness, Jacob was studying at his desk when the phone rang. He fingered the medal of the Black Madonna as he picked up the instrument and listened as a voice asked, "Are you Jacob Gorska?"

"Yes."

"Hello, Jacob. My name is Homer Cranston, and I'm with the State Department."

"The US State Department?" Jacob questioned.

"The same."

"I've been expecting your call."

"I am following up on the visas for Karyn Dietrich and her mother from East Germany. Sorry for the delays, but there are some issues."

"What are they?"

Homer answered, "Were you aware that Karyn's stepfather was a Nazi under suspicion of war crimes?"

"Are you sure? Karyn never talked about him."

"So it's no dice. I am sorry. The DDR won't issue their exit visas."

"What's that got to do with Karyn?"

"I am not sure, but that is what the DDR is telling us," Homer said.

Jacob said, "Are you sure you can't get the government to make an exception?"

"Fat chance. America and the Soviets are on the verge of war over the Berlin Wall."

"It makes no sense that Karyn is so important."

"Jacob, listen. You are against a stone wall, no pun intended—actually, the Iron Curtain. If I may give you some advice, get yourself a new life and a new girlfriend. We will not start an international incident in the name of love with a Nazi war criminal in her past."

"He hasn't been convicted."

"Jacob, please understand that we can't help you."

Jacob slammed the phone down as he shouted, "I won't wait." He then poured himself a drink from the bottle of Jack Daniels bourbon on his desk.

While Jacob sat brooding in his armchair five days later, he heard a gentle knock on his door. He opened it, drink in hand. Ryan Litchfield stepped in as he moved back and turned away. Tears slowly filled his eyes.

She asked, "What's going on with you?"

"Why are you here?"

"I came to see if you wanted to go to a hockey game. I'm leaving for Europe in a few days." When Jacob did not answer, she asked, "Is everything all right?" She glanced at the bottle of bourbon.

Jacob said, "This is not a good time, Ry."

Ryan stepped in front of him. "You've been crying and drinking too much again."

Ryan took the glass from Jacob and asked him to stand up. She hugged him. Jacob sobbed on her shoulder as he told her, "I can't get Karyn out of East Berlin."

"I am not surprised with what's happening over there. I've got an assignment to leave for Europe in three days to report on the brewing trouble in Germany."

Jacob stepped back and wiped his eyes. "Thanks, Ry, for being here."

"So now what will you do?" she asked.

"I am not sure. I guess work with George, sell lots of stocks, get rich, and wait until I die."

"You really sound deeply depressed."

"Of course not. My world suddenly turns to shit. What? Me worry?" Ryan moved against Jacob, put her hands behind his head, and pulled his lips to hers. "You want me to stay with you? It might help if I take you to another place."

Jacob pulled her tightly, and they kissed several times rapidly, rapidly removing each other's clothing. They touched each other, familiar passionate lovers tenderly caressing one another. Ryan soothingly stroked his hot, naked body, rocking him, and then they slowly began making love.

Finished, they lay quietly, their warm, glistening bodies touching, when Jacob said, "I wish you wouldn't go to Europe."

"It's a good career move. Come to Paris. We could live there together while you sort out your life."

"What about Karyn?"

"Are you crazy? She's history, darling."

"I am not so sure. I can try my congressman."

Ryan moved away from him. "And what about me—you and me?"

"I'm sorry. That was crass of me."

"Well, lover, make up your mind before I get bowled over by a Frenchman."

Jacob said, "Are you upset with me?"

"Of course not. What makes you think a silly thought like that? You only started to talk about Karyn right after we fucked. It wasn't even making love. Why would I be upset?"

"I thought you wanted me to be happy."

Ryan lifted herself from the bed and reached for her clothes. "You just wanted a good fuck."

"Don't get me wrong. Of course it was good. Was it good for you?"

Do Not Ask for a Reward

Alice, the Rallses' maid, took several letters from the mailman. She sorted through them before removing one. She walked up to Jacob's room and knocked on his door. As he opened the door, she handed him the letter. It bore an East Berlin return address. He recognized Karyn's handwriting and quickly ripped it open.

Darling Jacob,

How I have missed your letters when they don't come weekly.

Life continues as usual with work and diversions. I was told I can't compete anymore in ice skating competition because I am considered a flight-to-the-West risk. I guess if I were more talented, I wouldn't be banned. I don't really care because they are grooming skaters better than me for the Olympics.

So many people are leaving East Berlin. Many are shot dead trying. The borders are being closed more tightly each day. They say it is to protect us against an invasion from the West. I do not believe it.

Please let me know about the exit visa.

I love you, darling, and count the days until we will be together again.

Karyn, with kisses

Jacob sat quietly, limp as the letter dangled from his hand. His feeling of depression came slowly. How was he going to tell Karyn there would be no visas? It was then that he decided he had enough of life, but to pull himself out of the depressed mood, he decided to fly to Milwaukee on business, hoping the trip would buoy his spirits.

After meeting with several Milwaukee stock brokers to whom he introduced three of George Winslow's investment products, he went to visit a friend studying dentistry, but he was out of town. Next, he made a visit to Marquette University Jesuit Church of the Gesu located on the campus.

Once inside, he felt more relaxed and safer. He knelt close to the altar of the Gothic-style building so he could better see the artwork, the crucifix, and the painting of Mary with her son, Jesus. As he left the church and stepped onto Wisconsin Avenue, he heard his name called. He stopped and looked behind him to see it was Father Mickey McFarland.

The Jesuit priest said, "I knew I'd see you here."

"How did you know I was in Milwaukee?" Jacob questioned. "You truly are the hound of heaven."

"Martha Ralls told me you came for business."

"You're stalking me, Mickey."

"You have time for dinner?"

"Sure," Jacob agreed.

They were taken to a booth in the quieter area away from the traffic of patrons entering and leaving the Hotel Pfister Mason Street Grill. Once they were settled in, Jacob told the priest, "It's good seeing you again. How have you been?"

"I'm doing well. I heard you got some bad news from the US State Department. What's going on?"

Jacob explained, "I can't get Karyn an exit visa. Seems her stepfather was or is a Nazi war criminal."

"You didn't know?"

"Karyn never told me about him. How was I to know?"

"That is bad news."

They each ordered rib eye steaks, medium rare, which they ate while chatting about the past to bring themselves up to date on what had happened.

The priest reminded Jacob, "I told you something like this would happen. This is a sign from God that you have a calling and a religious mission. Your task now is to serve others as a part of his army."

"And, of course, join the Jesuits," Jacob added.

"Forget Karyn. Move on. Do the right thing for yourself and your parents. It's what they would have wanted, and you know that."

After they returned to the Jesuit residence, Jacob told Father McFarland about his past, including his visit to Italy and to Yugoslavia and how he met Karyn.

The priest told Jacob, "Put it behind you."

Jacob asked, "Will this affect my joining the order?"

"So you decided?"

"I need a little more time."

The priest said, "Don't take too much time. Satan is working on you."

Jacob asked for a blessing. Father McFarland placed his hands on Jacob's head and prayed, "Our Dear Heavenly Father, please console your son Jacob at his time of grief. Bless him that he will make the right decision to join the order and fulfill the mission and calling you have chosen for him. Bless him with the strength to do your will not his, to fight and not heed the wounds, to give and not count the cost, to toil and not seek rest, and to labor and not ask for reward except knowing that he is doing your divine will." They were the words of St. Ignatius Loyola who founded the Jesuit order.

Father McFarland fondly embraced Jacob. "Heavenly Father loves you, Jacob."

Jacob promised, "I'll give you an answer next week."

Father McFarland nodded and made the sign of the cross over Jacob before he left the room. And then the priest picked up the phone and dialed a number. "Hello, Father Superior. Set another place for dinner. Jacob Gorska will be joining us for the eternal feast."

Stop Feeling Sorry for Yourself,

Paris, 1961

Ryan Litchfield was in the Paris news department of the *International Herald Tribune* composing a news article on her IBM Selectric typewriter, trying to master the new intricate electric machine that replaced her manual Underwood. The newspaper plant and offices was located in a major business district called *la defense* just west of the city limits of Paris as part of the Paris Metropolitan area.

Her *International Herald Tribune* work location was four miles from where she had a small apartment. It was her seventh week working on her new assignment as a rewrite journalist who also had the job of investigative reporting on assignments all over free Europe.

She had a call on her direct line. She lifted the instrument and spoke her greeting into the mouthpiece and listened.

"Hi, Ry. It's Jacob."

"My God, darling, it's so good to hear a familiar voice. You in the city?" Ryan asked.

Jacob glanced at the letter from Karyn in his hand. "How I wish you were here. I have no one now."

Ryan tried hard not to be stern when she said, "I asked you to come here, so we could be together. Remember?"

Jacob picked up his drink. A quick mental flashback of his parents being murdered stopped him from speaking.

Ryan asked, "What's wrong. What do you mean you are alone?"

He glanced at the letter in his hand. "Karyn got married."

Ryan advised, "Don't become overreactive, darling. What did you expect? She'd wait until hell froze over?"

"I'm having a rough time ..." he said, his voice trailing off.

"Jacob, listen—you have to move on, or you'll drive yourself crazy."

Just then, her editor stopped at her desk and signaled he had to talk with her right away. He stood quietly but impatiently as he waited.

Ryan put her hand over the mouthpiece and said, "Sorry, Marcel. This is a personal call, and I'll be with you in a minute."

He pouted, nodded his head, and moved toward his office.

Jacob said, "She could have waited, couldn't she?"

Ryan said, "Come over here and fuck my brains out, and I guarantee you'll never think of that *fraülein* again."

"That's not funny, Ry."

"Not meant to be. Stop feeling sorry for yourself."

"Those commie pricks play hardball."

"What a damn surprise, fella. What else is new, eh? The Reds want to eat us for breakfast and save the leftovers for dinner."

"So how are you doing?" Jacob asked her.

"Fighting off a Parisian penis every day." She noticed her editor glaring at her. "I gotta go, lover."

"I'll get back to you," Jacob told her. "What's your home number?"

She gave it to him and added, "Don't lose that number, buster. I want to hear from you real soon."

Where Shall We Break Bread?

Later that afternoon, Jacob got a call from Father McFarland.

His spirits lifted. "Hey. Where are you?" Jacob asked.

"I'm out at Manresa preparing for a men's retreat."

"Are you giving or taking?"

The priest laughed. "Giving. How about dinner tonight? The Society will spring for the tab."

"I'd be delighted. Where shall we break bread?"

"Grosse Pointe Yacht Club? Say, eight?"

Jacob said, "I'll drive by for you. What's up?"

"Just staying in touch."

Jacob and McFarland sat at a window table with a view of Lake St. Clair and the running lights on the small sailboats slowly moving in and out of the marina. The priest made a mental note that Jacob was drinking a lot of wine.

"Sorry about Karyn, but you knew it was coming. You two did not have a future."

"You truly are the heartless hound of heaven," Jacob told him. "How did you find out?"

"Martha Ralls called me. She said you looked despondent and is worried about you. And besides, you told me you would give me an answer about this time. So what is it?"

Jacob smiled, "You're stalking me, Mickey."

"Not really, but I told you something like this would happen. These are signs from God that you have a calling and a mission in life."

"And I suppose you have a solution? Join the Jesuits?"

"Do the right thing. Like I said before, it's what your parents would have wanted, and you know that."

Jacob told him, "Ryan wants me to join her in Paris. I think I'll do just that."

"Why would you do that? More denial? More running from your vocation? More sex and booze?"

Jacob studied a moving green light on the river as he thought for a moment. "I am not sure, Mickey."

Mickey gently touched Jacob's arm and asked, "What else has life got to offer?"

"I am not sure."

"What are you sure of? The answer is not in sins of the flesh and booze. You drink too much because you're hurting inside."

"I'm not an alcoholic," Jacob said defensively.

"They all say that. Let me get help for you."

Jacob sighed. "Let's call it a night, Mickey. I have to get up early tomorrow."

Father McFarland put his arm around Jacob's shoulder as they walked out.

Jacob asked, "Why do you always see things in black and white, Mickey? It's not a Jesuit thing."

When Jacob stopped at the Jesuit residence, the priest said, "Let me know if there is anything I can do."

Assigned to the History Department

Jacob did not really like selling stocks and bonds. "I have to reinvent the wheel every day," he told Father McFarland on the way to the tennis club for a game. "Ford manufacturing doesn't interest me."

After the game, they showered and went to the grill for dinner.

The next day, Jacob decided he had no more excuses. He called McFarland, and within the week, he joined the Society of Jesus.

During the intake interview, Jacob admitted to the Jesuit interviewer his faults, poor choices, and past sins. He wanted to enter the community with a clean mind and heart, but also, it was to let Father Superior know in case there would be some issue down the road that might have to be addressed.

It was four years after Jacob entered the order. He was studying in his Jesuit seminary room when the bell for daily dinner sounded. He slowly dressed in his best cassock and left for the refractory. He hesitated before departing his room, wanting to take a drink of the rare malt scotch George Winslow had given him as a going-away present. But he decided it wouldn't look good if he had the odor of alcohol on his breath at dinner.

As he walked the quiet halls of the Jesuit residence, he recalled when he was new to the Jesuit order how the older priests hazed him a little as any fraternity brother would do to a pledge. The order was suppose be more dignified, but boys will be boys—even when they look like grown men. It was all harmless fun—another test of the man. He would in the future have his turn to haze.

He took his place at the dinner table and waited for Father Benjamin at the head of the table to begin the prayers. The food was already on the table and tempting, and everyone waited—another test of self- control. They were always challenging the body to help overcome carnal pleasures. Give in here, and later you give into another temptation. For Jacob, it was difficult being celibate at first, but as the years passed, he lost the urges.

"They didn't castrate us," he would jokingly tell anyone who asked.

Obedience was not such a problem. He learned at an early age to do what his parents wanted. His mother made sure he became dependent upon her without meaning him any harm. She would on occasion tell her friends she had just been looking out for the youngster's well-being.

The vow of poverty he easily accepted. He had entered the order with nothing, and his superiors provided him with whatever he needed to fulfill his calling, which is what the vocation needed. He was treated well, and in response, he gave all he could for the greater glory of God (*ad majorem dei Gloriam*, abbreviated AMDG—the motto of the order's founder Ignatius Loyola). Whenever he was given a gift, he had to go to his superior and ask for permission to keep it, and unless the society felt it needed the gift more than him, he was allowed to keep it

Jacob explained to Susan Ralls that a Jesuit wannabe priest spends about sixteen years preparing for his ordination, studying theology, philosophy, and other courses needed to obtain his baccalaureate and prepare him for ordination.

His father confessor advised him to seriously consider getting a doctorate in European history with an emphasis on Eastern Europe. "You could teach at the university level. You don't want to stay a lowly high school teacher, do you? Putting up with brats and such."

Jacob did get his PhD in Eastern European studies from Harvard University.

The order then assigned him to the history department of Marquette University.

He was ordained a Jesuit priest in 1977. Malcolm and Martha Ralls, joined by Ryan, Susan and her husband Ted along with father McFarland observed the ceremonies. Afterward the group went for dinner.

Two years later Jacob was installed as head of the history department for Marquette University.

The Secret Alliance

Shortly after his January 1981 inauguration, newly installed US president Ronald Reagan and Pope John Paul II held a secret afternoon telephone conference during which they discussed the political situation in Poland and how the country could be separated from the Soviet Union.

Reagan agreed with the pope. "The Yalta Agreement mistakes must be corrected."

The pope suggested, "Together we can help free Poland and use it as a weapon against Moscow's influence in Europe. We can be an influential factor in the equation."

Reagan promised, "I will use all my resources to this end."

The pope said he would arrange to get information from Poland, and through his many church sources, spread throughout the world. He was consecrated a bishop and became Archbishop of Krakow, Poland in 1958 during the era when the Soviet Union controlled the Polish Communist government after World War II. He knew many Poles who admired and believed in him and that they would cooperate to get from under the Kremlin oppression.

President Reagan asked, "Then we have an alliance?"

"Of course."

President Reagan had determined he would shut down the Soviets, and less than two weeks after his inauguration, he took his first action— he assembled in the Oval Office the senior members of his national security team. Present were: US vice president George H. W. Bush; national security adviser Richard Allen; CIA director William Casey; secretary of defense Caspar "Cap" Weinberger; and secretary of state Gen. Alexander Haig.

In a press conference, Weinberger later said that the group had decided there was a need to take a stand on Poland. The premise was to prevent an invasion of the country by Soviet troops and find ways to undermine Kremlin power in that country.

The president grabbed a handful of multicolored jelly beans from the bowl on his desk, leaned back in his high-backed chair, and asked with a bright smile, "Why do I feel outnumbered by Catholics?"

Casey laughed. "Because you are."

"So what pressing matters do you bring me?" the president asked.

Casey answered, "Pershing and cruise missiles in Europe."

Allen asked, "You still want them even with the geopolitical heat over there?"

"Damn right I do."

Gates said, "If it gets really hot over there, we'll be ready to offset any anti-American demonstrations."

The president opined, "The demonstrators are all sponsored by Moscow." He leaned forward, and with a grave expression on his face, he added, "Do you think the Soviets will invade Poland over this Solidarity thing?"

Gates answered that there was a fifty-fifty chance. "My guess is that the new Polish prime minister Wojciech Jaruzelski would instead suggest martial law."

Reagan said, "That hard-line son of a bitch just had to be appointed."

"Jaruzelski doesn't want the Soviets in town, and Moscow doesn't want to lose Poland."

Allen told the others, "Actually, Jaruzelski is the lesser of two evils. While he's a hard-liner, he's protective of his turf."

Reagan asked, "Even against Moscow?"

"Yes."

"One good thing is the majority of Poles are Catholic, and the pope is Polish."

Gates chuckled. "Boy, did the Kremlin flip over that situation. The Reds thought he was a Socialist and a friend of Communism."

Reagan added, "Well, like I say, there's always a pony buried under that pile of manure." He then told the group, "We also must send information and messages of encouragement to Lech Walesa, the leader of the free Polish workers' union, Solidarity."

They all knew that both the Kremlin and the Red Polish regime were nervous about the labor movement.

Casey looked at the president for a long time before he said, "You are known in some parts of the world as the Sheriff."

Reagan responded, "Am I?"

Gates added quickly, "One with a dream of shutting down the Communists."

Allen brought up another piece of business. The president told him to make it quick.

"The pope has suggested the name of a priest we can smuggle into Poland."

"Let's meet on that over breakfast. Does it look doable?" the president asked.

"Very, sir."

Casey concurred.

Allen asked, "You want to hear a good story?"

The president, always happy to hear them, nodded.

Allen continued, "This diplomat met with the pope and offered to tell him a Polish joke."

Reagan said, "This better be good."

"Well, the pope told him he was Polish. The diplomat then said, 'I'll tell it to you slowly.'"

Reagan laughed and told his visitors, "Better get out before Nancy walks in and asks what we're doing."

The Man from Poland, 1980

A cardinal and a man from Poland walked through the Portone di Bronzo entrance to the Vatican Apostolic Palace from the Belvedere courtyard. They walked to the Vatican library, officially the Vatican Apostolic Library, often called the VAT.

The two men joined the first Polish pope, John Paul II. The visitors were Cardinal Casaroli, the Vatican Secretary of State; and Lech Walesa, leader of Communist Poland's independent workers' union, Solidarity.

The cheerful pope, with a twinkle in his eye, smiled as he greeted them. His sturdy frame had the attributes of an athlete, the result of many hours in the exercise room of a gymnasium. His modest demeanor and his warm and personal manner put his visitors at ease.

Casaroli pointed to the front page news story of *La Repubblica*, a popular influential Italian newspaper, when he told Walesa, "You certainly attracted a lot of attention when you met with the head of the Italian Communist Party, Enrico Berlinguer."

Walesa reverently answered, "He backs our efforts to have a free Poland, and he publicly warned Moscow there would be the gravest consequences if there is military intervention."

"Anyway, Lech, we don't want to see a huge public relations coup for Solidarity."

The pope advised, "You must move carefully, Son. And don't be political. You are lucky prime minister Jozef Pinkowski and the government let you travel here."

The cardinal, who favoreddialogue with Moscow, agreed. "According to our intelligence, Moscow is very unhappy with such events."

Walesa answered in his defense. "Yes, but we must get the free world on our side."

"The free world understands," advised the pope. "But if things get too antagonistic for Moscow, they will replace Pinkowski with a more difficult hard-liner."

The Pole blinked and agreed. "That would be Minister of Defense Jaruzelski."

Cardinal Casaroli warned Walesa, "Yes. So see that you don't abuse your privileges."

Lech said, "With all respect, Your Imminence, travel and meeting with workers of other countries is a right and helps promote peaceful dialogue."

The pope was sympathetic. "True, but use discretion so you don't lose all the ground you have won."

The cardinal secretary warned, "You could find Poland under martial law. You don't want that."

"I make every effort to depoliticize my travels."

The pope suggested the group move on. He said, "We eagerly await the day Ronald Reagan becomes president of the United States this month."

"So," added the cardinal, "we must make it easy for him to help Poland. If you antagonize the Kremlin, then the Soviets will be more difficult."

"We can get what we want peacefully if we are patient," advised the pope. "We must show Moscow that the Catholic Church does not want political power."

Cardinal Casaroli said, "We want human rights respected, but we don't want the labor unions to look like Catholic organizations."

Walesa nodded. "I understand, but Poland remains in crisis."

"That's is true. Soviet General Secretary Brezhnev said publicly that he believes outside powers push Poland toward destruction."

The pope added, "The Soviet Ambassador recently met with me and urged continued restraint of Polish workers."

"Do we have your word you will follow this advice?" Casaroli asked.

Walesa gave his word. "But what if the situation changes for the worse?"

"We are formulating a plan in case that happens."

"Can you share this information with me?" Walesa asked.

"Not at this time. You will learn more in good time."

The pope said, "Lech, my son, you must trust me. I know what it's like. I lived under Nazi domination during the war in Poland, and later I was there when the Soviets took over. I lived under their oppression."

Obsession with Actress Jodie Foster

The Washington, DC, Hilton Hotel, also called the Hilton Washington, is a twelve-story building located at 1919 Connecticut Avenue on the boundary of Dupont Circle. It has been a regular venue for the White House Correspondents' Association dinner.

The weather on the afternoon of March 30, 1981, was clear and crisp as President Reagan left the hotel after delivering a luncheon address to AFL-CIO labor leaders and representatives. The venue was considered the safest in Washington because of the enclosed passageway called the Presidents Walk, which had been built for security after the 1963 assassination of President John F. Kennedy.

It was nearly two thirty in the afternoon as Reagan walked fifteen feet in front of and past a group of admiring onlookers who had not been screened by the Secret Service.

Suddenly, gunshots were heard. There were six in less than two seconds fired from a Rohm RG-14 .22 LR blue steel revolver fired by the hand of an unknown named John Hinckley Jr. It was later determined that the motive behind the attack was to impress actress Jodie Foster, for whom he had an obsessed fascination after seeing her in the 1976 film *Taxi Driver*.

The president had refused to wear a bulletproof vest, which was a common piece of attire. He had told his security agents he did not need it for the short walk of about thirty feet from his limousine to the hotel and back again through the protected walkway.

It was the sixth and final bullet that ricocheted off the armored side of the limousine and struck the president's left side under the armpit. It grazed a rib before settling in his lung, which partially collapsed, and stopping less than an inch from his heart. Three other persons in the president's group were shot but not fatally, including his press secretary, James Brady, who suffered a head wound and was restricted thereafter to a wheelchair.

Hinckley was grabbed, thrown to the ground, and arrested by the police.

At first, no one, including the president, knew that he had been shot, and the agents prepared to take him to the White House medical facilities, which Reagan preferred over an unsecured hospital. However, the president suddenly felt great pain, which he thought was caused by a cracked rib. But when he coughed up bright, frothy blood, the motorcade change course to nearby George Washington University Hospital. They arrived in less than five minutes.

Agents took Hinckley to a DC Police Department jail.

The surgery to remove the bullet from president Reagan lasted a little more than one hour. During this time, Defense Secretary Weinberger conferred with National Security Adviser Allen in the White House Situation Room on the question of why at that time there was more than the usual number of Soviet submarines off the Atlantic coast.

Allen talked about his concerns that possible scenarios involving Soviet invasion of Poland against the Solidarity movement might take place. It wasn't long before the Kremlin knew about the president's physical health condition and could take advantage of the situation.

Weinberger asked, "You think we should raise the military alert status without changing the DEFCON level?"

"Perhaps we should wait until we see if there is a need to rollout the military for defense against an invasion."

Weinberger later raised the military alert status.

The president returned to the Oval Office on April 25, and his first public appearance was on April 28 when he spoke before the joint houses of Congress to introduce his plan to cut spending, one of his campaign promises.

Indiana Jones with a
Roman Collar

Marquette University's campus is approximately two miles from the city center of Milwaukee and located on Wisconsin Avenue. The planners of the evening event estimated no fewer than sixty people would attend Father Gorska's presentation in the Varsity Building lecture hall.

Outside the venue door stood an easel holding a sign that invited visitors to the activity:

> Father Jacob Gorska, SJ, MA, PhD
> Delivers His Research Findings
> *Eastern Europe History Today*

Inside the hall, Father Jacob stood before a whiteboard on which he wrote his thoughts in multicolored dry-erase words and phrases. His audience was mostly made up of students from the college, including some who were in the European history class. Jacob's specialty was history, particularly Eastern Europe with an emphasis on his native Poland. He had received numerous awards and grants for his work.

He was at the center of the large, otherwise empty stage that let the audience focus on him and his whiteboard. A television camera delivered his images onto a large overhead monitor that gave the attendees a better view of the speaker and his PowerPoint illustrations.

One of his students had dubbed him Indiana Jones with a Roman collar. He was very popular with his students, and he enjoyed the comfortable American academic life of a handsome, physically fit professor in his forties over whom coeds swooned in vain.

After he finished his lecture, Jacob announced there would be a brief intermission before he answered questions. A woman smartly dressed in a business suit approach the speaker. Wanda was the history department secretary.

"I'm sorry, Father, to interrupt," she said, "but there are two men who say it's urgent that they talk with you immediately."

"What do they want?" Jacob asked.

"I am not sure. They said they're from the government and it's a highly secret matter."

"What government?"

"The US government."

"They'll have to wait," Jacob told her.

Wanda asked, "How long?"

"Fifteen minutes. Put them in my office."

The two government agents waited impatiently. Wanda had led them to Jacob's outer office conference room and told them, "Father Gorska can see you in about fifteen minutes upon completing a lecture. He's a very busy priest."

The two agents looked around the room at the awards and other documents on the wall.

Agent Phillips, tall and sporting a flattop haircut, said, "Did you know this guy got the Pulitzer Prize for his textbook on East European history?"

Moore answered, "A regular Michael Kammen."

"Who the hell is is that?"

"He's a Pulitzer Prize winner for history. People of Paradox: An Inquiry Concerning the Origins of American Civilization."

Phillips said, "Never heard of him."

"That's because you only read comic books." Changing the subject, Moore added, "And here's a signed letter from the pope congratulating him on his Polish research."

Phillips said, "I see now why we're talking with this guy."

At that moment, Father Jacob walked into the room.

Agent Moore, a shorter, heavyset man with black hair that covered his ears and parted in the middle of his head, said, "Father, thank you for seeing us. I am Agent Moore, and this is Agent Phillips."

Jacob shook hands with the men. "Now what's this fuss all about?"

The men showed their CIA credentials.

Agent Phillips said, "You're quite a scholar of Polish history, present and past."

Jacob smiled and said, "I doubt you came all the way here to tell me that."

"You're right. Can we talk where it is more private?"

The priest ushered them into his office and closed the door. "Why all the secrecy?" he asked.

Agent Phillips told him that what they were about to discuss was highly classified and must not be repeated.

Jacob said, "I still don't understand."

Agent Moore said, "Bill Casey, the CIA chief, personally sent us here."

Agent Phillips added, "Also, President Reagan."

"And Pope John Paul II."

"Any really important people send you guys here?" Jacob sarcastically questioned.

"The pope and President Reagan think that with your help we can assist the Solidarity movement in Poland to get the Poles their freedoms and independence, and then they will serve as a weapon against Moscow."

Jacob warned, "You have to be cautious, or you'll force the Kremlin to send troops into Poland."

Agent Phillips said, "That's why we have this job for you."

"You want me to say a novena for the conversion of Russia?"

Agent Moore said, "Casey and the president want you to go to Poland."

Agent Phillips said, "They are counting on you to carry information and messages to Lech Walesa."

Jacob laughed. "Wait a minute. I'm not going on any trip to Poland."

As if he did not hear, Phillips said, "And when you return, you will bring important information back to us."

"You have the wrong person." He stood to signal the meeting was over. "I really must get to my work."

Moore told him that he was the only one qualified for such a mission.

"I am in no condition to meet such a hardy challenge."

Phillips told him, "In two days, you leave for special training at Fort Bragg, North Carolina."

"Why? They train killers there."

Moore answered, "Yes, but, Father, you'll learn how to survive."

Jacob sat down. "I just can't do that. Even if I want to oblige, I would need permission from our Jesuit society general in Rome."

"We already have his permission in writing, as well as from the pope."

"Well, I'm a priest, not a spy."

"You won't be spying in the usual sense," said Phillips.

Moore added quickly, "Your job will be as a messenger or courier between the pope and the Polish people, as well as a messenger from President Reagan."

"Well, you can forget about me doing your dirty work. You have professionals for this."

Phillips said, "The pope needs someone with your qualifications."

Jacob laughed. "I can just see the poster. The pope dressed in red, white, and blue, pointing a finger toward the viewer over the caption 'Uncle Karol needs you.'"

Moore asked, "So you will disobey the pope?"

"You got me there," Jacob admitted. "I took a vow of obedience."

"Don't you want to avenge your parents' murders?" Moore noted.

"Don't try to blackmail me with guilt," Jacob said. "That was thirty-three years ago. You go find the killer."

Agent Phillips told Jacob he would file his report with his CIA superiors and endorse the priest for the mission.

The CIA agents stood and shook Jacob's hand. "It's a done deal, Padre." Agent Moore said, "Have a nice trip to Rome."

As he watched the agents depart, Father Jacob thought that perhaps he might help locate the man who killed his parents and let the government mete out justice.

They Don't Let Priests in There

Father Jacob Gorska, dressed in the traditional flowing Jesuit black sutan, sat across the desk from his provincial superiors, Father Lawrence Garvey and Father Edward Stein.

Father Garvey said, "We agreed with the pope to send you to Poland as the pope's emissary to work with Lech Walesa and Solidarity."

Jacob said, "They don't let priests in there."

"As far as they are concerned, you are not a priest," Father Garvey pointed out.

"They'll kill me if the police find out what I'm doing."

Father Stein told him, "Don't worry, my son. The CIA and Solidarity will protect you."

Oh yeah, Jacob thought to himself.

Father Garvey added, "Remember, Son, you are a soldier of Christ in the truest tradition of St. Ignatius Loyola. We must fight the destroyer of freedom and justice."

"I'll do my best."

"That's the spirit. We knew we could count on you."

Jacob thought to himself, *I really had no option.*

After Jacob exited the room, Father Garvey said, "He may be the best candidate for the mission, but we all know how clever and ruthless the Soviets are."

"We have to trust in the Lord."

"And it's what the pope requested of another Pole. But it will give Father Gorska something new and meaningful to do."

Jacob was invited to an audience with Pope John Paul II in the pontiff's study. He entered the Vatican Palace and was escorted by a Swiss palace guard to the study shortly after his meeting with his Jesuit superior general.

That evening, Jacob called his mentor, Father McFarland, who asked, "Well, what did our Holy Father have to say?"

"He thinks I'm a super priest who can just wiggle my way through that Communist nest of vipers."

"Where is your faith?" McFarland replied. "You must trust in God."

Jacob angrily said, "I can't go back. Why do they make me?"

"You're ideally suited for the mission. You know the country and the language like a native."

"I am a native," Jacob pointed out.

"And this is your chance to avenge your parents' murders and help crush the Communists who are abusing the country of your ancestors."

"Yeah. That's what the CIA guys said."

"The pope does not do whimsy."

"You always were manipulative, Mickey."

His friend smiled. "Only for the greater glory of God. Go back and confront the demons that have been torturing you. It will do you good."

As Jacob hung up the phone, he thought, *Maybe.* The concept intrigued him to think that by going back he could find peace and freedom from his depression and too much alcohol by dealing with a moment of truth at last.

He sent a letter to Ryan telling her that he thought he was a little closer to resolving his problems.

"I am firmly determined to go on my mission," he wrote.

The Assassin

The shooter had vowed in 1979 to kill the pope, head of the universal worldwide Roman Catholic Church.

Following is information contained in police records which were based on a series of interviews with the shooter, a Turkish man named Ağca.

Beginning in August 1980, Ağca, under the alias of Vilperi, began crisscrossing the Mediterranean region, changing passports and identities, thus hiding his point of origin in Sofia, Bulgaria.

He entered Rome on May 10, 1981, coming by train from Milan. According to Ağca's later testimony, he met with three accomplices in Rome, one a fellow Turk and two Bulgarians. The assassination operation was commanded by Zilo Vassilev, the Bulgarian military attaché in Italy.

Ağca said that he was assigned this mission to assassinate Pope John Paul II by Turkish Mafioso Bekir Çelenk in Bulgaria. [2] According to Ağca, he and the backup gunman Oral Çelik were to open fire on the pope in St. Peter's Square and escape to the Bulgarian Embassy under the cover of the panic generated by a small planned explosion.

On the afternoon of May 13, 1981, Vatican visitors sat in St. Peter's Square, writing postcards and trading gossip while waiting for the pope to arrive. At last, Pope John Paul II appeared riding in the Fiat popemobile, and as the pope passed through an adoring and excited crowd at 5:17 p.m., he reached out and touched as many of the thousands of people as he could.

Ağca fired fourshots froma 9 mm Browning Hi Powersemiautomatic handgun with a 15 round magazine. The shooting critically wounded the pope. All four bullets hit him; two tore through his garments and lodged in his lower intestine, just missing his aorta, while the other two hit his left index finger and right arm.

Also injured were two bystanders: a woman from Buffalo, New York, was struck in the chest, and another was slightly wounded in the arm.

The planned small explosion never took place, and the shooter fled the scene of shocked onlookers and tossed the handgun under a truck. He was quickly grabbed by Vatican security chief Camillo Cibin who was helped by a nun and several spectators, thus preventing the Bulgarian from escaping.

The pope was immediately rushed to the *Policlinico Gemelli Hospital* in Rome, while the authorities combed the site for evidence. Çelik, the accomplice, panicked and fled without setting off his bomb or opening fire.

At the time, President Reagan was recovering from his own assassination attempt in Washington, DC, on March 30, 1981. When President Reagan returned to Washington after convalescing from his gunshot wound, he met with his CIA Director Casey, Deputy Director Gates, and National Security Adviser Allen in the Oval Office.

President Reagan met over lunch with CIA Director Casey; CIA deputy director Robert Gates; and National Security Adviser Allen. Afterward, they moved to the Oval Office with its windows overlooking the south lawn. The visitors sat on the two sofas at the north end near the fireplace in front of the president's large oak desk made from the timbers of the British exploration ship *Resolute*. It had been a gift from England's Queen Victoria to President Rutherford B. Hayes in 1880.

Allen brought up another piece of business. "The pope has suggested the name of a priest we can smuggle into Poland."

"Let's meet on that over breakfast. Does it look doable?"

"Very, sir."

The Right Person for the Mission

On a bright Wednesday morning, President Reagan sat across from CIA chief Bill Casey at the breakfast table in the Oval Office. He asked if Casey had any news about the alliance he had forged with Pope John Paul II. The scheme would help Solidarity and the oppressed people of Poland gain their civil rights and other freedoms.

Casey told the president, "We found just the right person we can smuggle into Poland."

"We lost the last priest in Poland. Did we ever find out why?"

"It's still being investigated."

"I hope he's one of your best agents this time with plenty of experience in Eastern Europe."

"He's a priest."

Reagan moved forward in his chair. "What?"

"It's what the pope wants."

"They'll kill him just like they did the last priest."

Casey explained, "Since then, we have increased our clandestine operations in Poland. He'll be protected."

The president wanted to know when and how this improved situation came about.

Casey explained, "We moved ahead to check out the candidates we all thought might be suitable."

"He's the Polish scholar from Marquette University?" asked Reagan. "Father Jacob Gorska."

"That's him. He was born in Poland and has been in America since he was fourteen years old. He's an American now."

Reagan said, "He'll be awfully green."

"As we speak, he's training at Fort Bragg to get the survival skills he needs for his mission."

Reagan said, "Well, I guess all we can do is see how he turns out. You make sure this covert operation has a high level of probable success."

"Yes, sir. He's the man. He'll fit in. We won't send him until he's ready."

President Reagan said, "You know I'll have to do a finding and sign an executive order for such a covert operation."

"I'll have the proper paperwork drawn up. After you sign it, I'll see it goes over to the Hill for Congress to digest and approve. Secretary of state Alex Haig can take care of that."

Reagan went on. "Now, let's talk about the significance of the Soviet and East German forces on maneuvers. Think they'll invade Poland?"

"Not any time soon. Just some saber rattling for local consumption to scare the Poles and convince them to not cause any trouble."

"Yeah. It keeps the populace from thinking about their terrible predicament." Reagan paused. "Well, I don't want another Prague Spring."

"Not a chance."

"And I want a daily top-secret briefing on this priest."

Casey told Reagan, "We will certainly do that, sir. I will personally deliver the briefings to you."

A year later, Pope John Paul II and President Reagan held a secret meeting in the Vatican library where they discussed the political situation in Poland and the latest plans for how the Soviet Union could be dismantled.

President Reagan vowed again he was more determined than ever to shut down the Soviets.

It's Crunch Time

A squad of soldiers in fatigues stood at attention outside their Fort Bragg barracks when Company Commander Brian Criddle reviewed them. Jacob Gorska was in the second line. After all were accounted for, Criddle turned to the NCO next to him and handed him the clipboard of names. "They're all yours, Sergeant."

Master Sgt. Burton Johnson shouted in clipped fashion. "At ease. You are here to learn self-confidence. We will teach you both physical and mental endurance. You will learn to win close-combat encounters and how to neutralize your enemy." He paused. "Okay, ladies. Right face, forward march."

The first thing the company commander had done was order Jacob Gorska into the hand-to-hand combat training area. Observing were Battalion Commander Col. F.R. Sibert and his aide Lt. Doris Wynn. Next to them were CIA agents Moore and Phillips.

"Who's that clumsy guy over there?" Wynn asked, pointing to Jacob.

"Doris, you wouldn't know it, but that man is a priest."

Doris asked, "What's a priest doing here?"

The colonel said, "Special orders from the top to get him in shape within in the next two months."

The lieutenant choked. "He's too old. He won't make it."

"He's got to."

Agent Moore told her, "And it's your job to make sure he gets in shape by the end of this month."

She told the agent, "The priest doesn't look like he's assertive enough to attend assertiveness training classes."

"That's your problem."

She clinched her jaw, squinted her eyes, and looked a long time at the agents. "Who in hell are you guys anyway?"

Sibert informed her, "They're CIA. Ordered here by our commander in chief. Got a problem with that?"

"No, sir. I definitely do not."

The group watched in silence as Jacob successfully defended himself against a bayonet attack.

She asked her boss, "Why is he here?"

Colonel Sibert shrugged, "We have not been told except that it's some special assignment. You should see his file. He's as good as any."

Agents Moore and Allen said nothing while Jacob threw his cane shaped baston through the air at tremendous speed until it hit its target; the action created a whistling sound.

The lieutenant said, "He looks really good at this hand-to-hand Filipino Kali and Arnis combat."

Sibert said, "Exactly what we need. Where he's going he won't have any weapons except his body, his wits, and the knowledge he learns here."

Wynn said, "I read his file, and it says he will also get pilot training.

What does that mean?"

"All options are on the table. One of them is flying in an ultralight aircraft."

She looked puzzled. "And you don't know where he's going?"

"Oh, I know, but it's top secret. All you need to know is that he has to be trained like a soldier and be able to fight like a soldier in eight weeks." Sibert looked at her. "If you have anything to say, say it now."

"Yikes."

Covert Policy Trumps Foreign Policy

Bob Woodward of the *Washington Post* wrote: "Covert policy overrode implied US foreign policy; it was a fundamental component of President Reagan's activist foreign policy to thwart Marxist activities."

Some covert action took place in Eastern Europe, including the USSR and Poland. President Reagan approved covert support for the Polish labor movement Solidarity.

A high-level covert action screening committee was created at the urging of CIA Director Casey. He called it the National Security Planning Group, a subcommittee of the National Security Council. The Council included the vice president, the secretaries of state and defense, the president's national security adviser, the CIA director, the president's chief of staff, the presidential counselor, and the deputy chief of staff. It was the only group authorized to consider covert action programs to prevent leaks. Under its special activities category, the president was able to approve Father Gorska's covert mission in Poland.

In order to effect this mission, Reagan transmitted to the CIA a directive to generate proposals for a possible covert action. Once the operational and supporting details were worked out, a draft called the Presidential Finding was generated. After that, a proposal was investigated by the Covert Action Review Group, and once this group concurred, including final approval by the general counsel with respect to legal issues, the proposal was then passed up to the CIA for transmittal to the White House.

After the administration carefully and extensively reviewed the proposal and felt it was ready, a finding was signed by Reagan and sent to the intelligence committees of Congress. The finding had to be prepared with supporting documents, including a plan of action, risk assessment, and any resources required from the Department of Defense in support as required for the program. In the finding, the president stated that he found the proposal to be in the security interests of the United States and that it would be an operation of the CIA.

Soon after Reagan signed the necessary executive order to send Jacob to Poland as covert operation, code: **Butterfly**, Jacob packed his bags and prepared for his trip to Italy where he would make his final preparations before clandestinely entering Poland.

It Is God's Will

The Alitalia Boeing 747 took fourteen hours en route to deliver Jacob at Rome's Leonardo da Vinci-Fiumicino Airport where he was met by a Vatican State Department priest.

"Hope your trip was enjoyable," said Father Stein while the two walked from the baggage carrousel. Father Stein had the build of a rugby player, as he had played in college. He had a small nose and prominent lips, and he talked in a soft voice with hesitations. He insisted on carrying Jacob's bag.

"The flight was tedious and uneventful."

"My car is parked close by."

Actually, it was at the curb. A short, attractive, blonde policewoman stood next to it. She greeted them by saying, "Buon giorno padre." Then she bowed, turned, and moved on.

Jacob was curious. "What was that all about?"

"The car has diplomatic status, and she was kind enough to watch it for me."

It was a short drive to the Vatican apartment in a building across a walkway from the garden bordering the Basilica of St. Peter's where Father Stein showed Jacob his room.

"Dinner will be in two hours. And please stay awake. Jet lag is no excuse."

The next day Jacob met with the Society's superior general, and fathers Garvey and Stein. The superior general asked Jacob, "Do you have any questions about your mission?"

"I think I understand most of it. What I don't understand is why you think I am good enough for the task."

Father Stein told him, "You will succeed because it is God's will."

Jacob remained silent, thoughtful.

The superior general of the Jesuits sat across a walnut table from Jacob. He was elderly, stooped slightly when he stood, and had shiny naturally silver-colored hair. He spoke quietly to Jacob when he said, "Jacob, under no circumstances are you to go to East Germany."

Father Garvey added, "Especially East Berlin."

Jacob quietly blinked.

Father Stein continued, "Nor are you to contact Karyn Dietrich."

Both priests studied Jacob's reaction and waited for his reply.

Jacob said, "Of course I will not contact her. She's not a part of my life anymore, and I don't even know where she is."

The superior general smiled. "You leave from Rome in two days for Poland."

"I'll be landing at Warsaw?"

"No. You parachute into a landing zone outside the city of Gdansk.

Polish secret police should not know you have arrived."

The priests stood and shook hands, and Jacob left the room alone.

The superior general said, "We must pray for Jacob. The devil is close and grasping for his soul."

It was a Friday morning in Rome when Jacob met with Cardinal Agostino Casaroli, Ted Fontaine, and Father Garvey. Ted had founded his company in the Silicon Valley of California adjacent to San Jose in the city of Menlo Park. He called his company Microdatronics; the enterprise made computer chips and computer-driven devices. Some people called him the other "Wizard of Menlo Park".

Ted put onto the table what looked like a small cigar case. "This is a text scanner and computer built into this cigar case."

He opened the case, revealing four foul-smelling cigars. He removed the cigars and gently pried the bottom off the case to reveal an electronic device.

Ted explained, "Pass this device over a document, and it files the images in the computer memory, which you can transmit to Rome through a satellite or bring back with you the information for President Reagan and the pope."

The cardinal said, "Amazing what God can do."

Ted smiled. "We did this, Father, with technology from God."

"I won't argue that point."

Jacob asked, "How can I transmit?"

Ted drew a diagram to explain the data burst concept. In telecommunication, a burst transmission or data burst is the broadcast of a relatively high-bandwidth transmission over a short period of time. Broadcasting a compressed message at a very high data signaling rate within a very short transmission time is popular with the military and spies, who both wish to minimize the chance of their radio transmissions being detected. There is a low probability of intercept and low probability of recognition.

In the 1980s, the term *data burst* was used for a technique to transmit large amounts of primarily textual information. Multiple pages of text would be displayed in rapid succession.

"We will equip you with a special radio that you can use to send information in short signal bursts. That way they cannot be intercepted."

Book 3

The Black Aircraft

In an airport hangar far away from the Rome passenger terminal building sat a black aircraft with a matte finish and no markings. It was leased by the CIA, the major intelligence organization for the United States of America; the single-engine plane was used frequently for clandestine missions.

Ciampino Airport (Aeroporto di Roma-Ciampino), or G. B. Pastine Airport, was an important civilian, commercial, and military airport near Rome, Italy. Ciampino Airport was opened in 1916 and is now one of the oldest airports still in operation.

During World War II, the airport was captured from German troops by Allied forces in June 1944 and afterward became a US Army Air Forces military airfield. Although primarily used as a transport base by C-47 Skytrain aircraft of the Sixty-Fourth Troop Carrier Group, the Twelfth Air Force Eighty-Sixth Bombardment Group flew A-36 Apache combat aircraft from the airport during the immediate period after its capture.

It was later opened by the Italian government to commercial air traffic with the introduction of Ryan Air and Iceland Air services. Ciampino Airport became a popular alternative to the heavily congested Leonardo Da Vinci International Airport.

As the pope was recovering from his gunshot wounds in the *Policlinico Gemelli Hospital* in Rome, the black Cessna Centurion departed the city at sundown and flew during a moonless night over the West German countryside. The pilot double-checked to be sure he had activated the autopilot before he turned to look at Jacob Gorska seated behind him.

Jacob looked at the blackness through the open space where the right-hand passenger door had been removed and through which he would jump with his parachute strapped to his back.

The pilot told Jacob he would let him know when to unsnap his seat belt and get ready for the jump. The plane was at that time less than one hour from the East German border with Poland. The Polish underground fighters would meet Jacob and safely guide him to his destination of Gdansk, Poland.

Jacob saw the fires of the landing zone in the distant dark farmland below. As they flew closer, the pilot said, "Now you jump. And good luck, Padre."

The men and women of the partisan underground had prepared a landing zone for Jacob by setting several fires in a large circular area. They looked up as the airplane flew overhead at a height of 1,500 feet. They could barely see Jacob's opened parachute in the blackness of the night as it glided down, missing the landing zone and going into tree branches.

He worked quickly to untangle the lines and get out of the chute harness. As he was climbing down, he saw two dark figures with rifles pointed toward him.

A man named Alfons asked, "Who's the best quarterback?"

Jacob answered with the correct code word. "Joe Namath."

Alfons's group helped Jacob to the ground. "Welcome to Poland, Father Jacob. Follow us. I am Alfons. These friends are Stefania, Edmund, and Wicenty."

Jacob and his new friends ran from the landing zone site. They carried backpacks and were headed to Gdansk, the birthplace of Solidarity. Alfons told Jacob, "When we get to the outskirts of Gdansk, you must change into the clothes of a dock worker. Our men will meet you, take you to the docks, and get you working."

They stopped just long enough to bury the parachute, and Jacob asked if anyone had water. He greedily drank from the canteen that Stefania handed to him as the others folded the parachute into a small package to bury. Alfons stopped his companions with a motion to be quiet.

Polish secret police walked through the woods near the spot where Jacob had landed. Alfons's group quickly disappeared into the forest's denser brush just as the police searched Jacob's landing area.

The lead officer said, "I know the parachute came down here. Look where they lit the fires. Shoot anything that moves."

One of the group pointed and said, "They went farther into the woods."

The hunters rushed into the trees after Alfons's group.

Partisans were able to reach a safe area where Alfons told Jacob that he would lead him to a car that would take him to the northern city of Gdansk known to the Germans as Danzig—the same city where the Nazis invaded Poland in 1939 to start World War II. Once at Gdansk, he would meet with other underground members.

Alfons advised, "Once safely inside the city, you can meet with Solidarity and complete your mission."

With that, they left the area.

A Job for You at the Shipyard

Jacob and Alfons sat in the back of a Gdansk cafe on the old market square. Looking across the tables through the windows Jacob observed the darkness of the sky showing a hint of imminent rain. The citizens moved around rapidly to the various stores for their weekly shopping. Because the Germans had focused their activities farther south, the country had been spared the brunt of the war after the initial attack. Automobiles and wagons made pounding sounds as they traveled the stone streets.

Norbert joined Jacob's group. He was introduced as a member of the Solidarity movement. He told Jacob, "Here is your Polish ID with new name. We have a job for you at the shipyard for your cover."

Jacob told him, "Don't you think that it would be better if I hide until I meet Lech Walesa before returning to Rome?"

"Let's think about that. Meanwhile, you can stay at my house."

Jacob asked, "Is it safe?"

"As safe as any place in Poland." He and Jacob then left the café and began walking to Norbert's house.

We Need Help

Shortly after Jacob's arrival in Poland, a KGB officer from Moscow flew into the city, resulting in a tense meeting in Warsaw, Poland. The officer met with the local secret police to investigate the rumor that a stranger had recently parachuted into the country. KGB Col. Evgeny Biroschnikov questioned officers about what they had actually seen.

He was a pudgy man with a bent nose and very little hair left on his head. Most notable was the scarlet coloration on this right cheek, but it was brighter than before he vigorously started interrogating his hosts.

His voice was highly elevated when he asked, "So what do you actually know about somebody landing in Poland? And this person is supposedly now somewhere in the country, but you're too stupid to know where?"

The secret police officer who led the search of the landing area answered, "Sorry, Comrade. We don't know more than that."

"So why can't you take care of this? Why did you notify Moscow?"

"We needed help."

Biroschnikov shouted back, "Moscow thinks you shouldn't, but you do, and that's why I was sent here. Russian soldiers should have never left your goddam country."

"You are always welcome, Comrade."

Biroschnikov shouted, "We should have ten thousand Soviet soldiers here. Then this place would be secure."

"Sorry about that, Comrade."

Biroschnikov laughed. "I'm sure you're sorry, but wait until I find out what's really going on. Then you'll see what sorry truly means."

A policeman entered the room and was handing a message to the secret police agent when Biroschnikov grabbed it from the messenger and read it. He told the group, "Now I learn the invader is in Gdansk."

"Who is it?"

Biroschnikov answered, "It doesn't say. Maybe it's President Reagan. Imbeciles. They are still trying to find out. Call the Gdansk commander and tell him to put all his men into the field. I want a report from those agents by the time I get there. Tell him to check the houses for strangers and report any new, unknown visitors. This alien will need a cover. Do these things immediately."

An officer asked, "You think this has to do with Solidarity?"

"What else? The crafty workers are always making trouble. You have to double your surveillance of all Solidarity members. We have to find the names of those underground enemies aiding foreign invading agents."

"I thought the church told Lech Walesa to back off and let the politicians negotiate their worker grievances."

Biroschnikov banged his fist on the desk. "Lech Walesa will do it his way. And the fucking pope doesn't want Walesa to fail."

Working at the Lenin Shipyard

Jacob Gorska, disguised in peasant work clothing, sat at a rustic wooden table in the Lenin Shipyard cafeteria with five other men and a woman, all dressed similarly, talking, looking at a map, drinking coffee, smoking, and laughing. The leader, Alfons, began making introductions.

Thanks to the false documents provided by solidarity, Jacob was working on the docks of the Lenin Shipyard in Gdansk. At first, he had resisted the idea of working there, out of fear that the police would discover him and end the mission he had been assigned by Pope John Paul II. After Alfons had explained the situation with Solidarity, Jacob decided he had to get inside the yards to meet the man who was working closely with Lech Walesa and waiting for a contact from the pope.

"This is Stefania," Alfons told him.

Stefania said, "You can call me Steffi if you like."

Alfons then introduced the others: "Edmund, Fryderyk, and Wicenty."

Wicenty told Jacob, "Call me Vinny. I am the tough guy."

Jacob said to Alfons, "I'll call you the Fonz."

"You're the boss, Father."

They all laughed and toasted each other.

During the first day working beside other dock workers in Gdansk, a man pulled Jacob aside. "I am Filip." He handed a folded paper to Jacob and said, "Go here tonight. Eight sharp. The code word is *stolik*. Memorize the address and then destroy the paper. There are spies everywhere."

Jacob looked around and put the paper into his pocket.

The man who called himself Filip quickly disappeared. Across the shipyard, a man observed the meeting and walked out of the factory. His destination was the police station.

That night at the assigned time, Jacob checked his watch and the address, saw it was the one he wanted, and after scanning the area carefully, he walked up to the door. He paused and knocked.

A woman answered through the door. "Who is it?"

Jacob answered. "Stolik."

She opened the door. "I am Elzbieta." She carefully bolted the door with three locks before leading Jacob up a flight of creaky wooden stairs. He was ushered into an undecorated room where seated around a table were Norbert and Filip, the man who had earlier given Jacob the note with the address.

Norbert beckoned Jacob to a chair at the head of the table. "Welcome, Father Jacob. Hey, Filip, pour our guest a drink."

Jacob took his seat as Filip placed a bottle of vodka and a glass in front of him. Jacob took a drink. "This is good."

Alfons laughed. "Made by the Soviets. We couldn't get any sacramental wine."

Norbert chided Alfons and asked Jacob, "You have information for us?"

"Yes, and I brought money. The supplies you want will arrive at Gdansk from Denmark and Sweden in mismarked containers." Jacob took Polish and American money from his pouch and handed the bills to Norbert.

He told the group, "Here are messages from the pope and American president Ronald Reagan. These tell what you can expect in the way of assistance and what is expected of Solidarity."

There was murmuring around the table and nods of assent as Jacob handed the package of messages to Norbert.

Jacob asked, "What about the report on the Polish government for the pope?"

Edmund produced a file. He said, "These are secret records of Polish government decisions and communications between Warsaw and Moscow. There are also our plans for strikes and peaceful demonstrations."

Jacob removed the scanner device from his bag, removed the cigars, and ran it over the papers.

Norbert asked, "What are you doing?"

"I'm recording the reports into a computer for digital transmission to the pope. I'll scan all reports. It's too dangerous carrying bulky papers."

Norbert handed Jacob a package and said, "Take this to Holy Father. It explains what we do here to win freedom. Is Holy Father pleased with our progress?"

"Yes, and he asks that you move forward without bringing the Soviets down on your heads by being political."

Alfons suggested, "We cannot just stand by idly."

Jacob said, "He means be careful and work within the system."

"Like in Hungary and Czechoslovakia?"

Norbert explained, "Lech Walesa wants us to be persistent in our strikes and state our main social rights demands."

Jacob advised, "You must remind the Reds that Poland is not their country but a Catholic country devoted to Jesus Christ and Pope John Paul II and a land of independence and liberties. Let the Communist regime in power know this."

Norbert asked, "Does he think the Soviet leaders will respect that?"

"Yes. The Kremlin not only respects, but fears the pope."

"Are you saying that we need approval by the Red authorities?"

"Yes. If you will be patient, you will get the approval. Move too quickly, and Jaruzelski and gang will strongly resist your demands and move against Solidarity."

It was Alfons who said, "You can tell the Holy Father we will not falter and let the Communists get the best of us."

Norbert added, "The commies have been exhausting our country.

It has to stop."

Jacob promised to carry his information back to Rome and President Reagan.

During Norbert's meeting, two cars pulled up in front of the house, and three men walked up to the door. Norbert heard them and went to the window. Seeing the cars, he told the group, "It's our friends the police again."

There was a loud banging on the entry door downstairs.

Filip said, "You must hide right away in case you have been followed. Elzbieta, take Jacob down the secret steps immediately. Follow the plan we devised. Jacob must not be caught."

Norbert told Filip, "Answer the door but stall the pigs. Joke with them. Anything."

Two men stood in the shadows across the street from Norbert's house. One told the other, "Our comrade chief will be very interested in what we see."

The other man agreed. "It should be good for special privileges."

They were agents for the KGB and Colonel Biroschnikov. One held a camera and had taken pictures of Jacob entering Norbert's house.

They walked away.

What Filip could not see were policemen in the shadows with weapons. The banging on the door intensified as the squad leader shouted, "Open up. Police."

Filip asked, "Who is it?"

"I told you, idiot. The police. Open up, or we break down this door."

"Just a minute." He pretended to be having trouble with the lock mechanism.

"Hurry up, imbecile."

Eventually, Filip opened the door. The policemen rushed in and shoved him against the wall as they ran to the stairs. One of the soldiers hit Norbert's gut with his gun stock and shouted, "Bastard."

Elzbieta had taken Jacob through a concealed ground-level door and led him out onto a narrow lane between two buildings. They ran to another house. Clara, holding a rifle, greeted them and led them upstairs. Her black hair was pulled tight and covered with a blue bandana. She did not smile but was conscious of all that was taking place.

When they were safely inside, Clara said, "You will be safe here."

Jacob asked, "Then what?"

Elzbieta told him, "Eventually, we'll get you to East Germany where the CIA will help you escape to the West."

He told her, "I can't go to East Germany."

"We will figure something that will work."

Clara told him, "You can stay here only two days. Then we have to move you."

"So I shouldn't get too settled."

"Exactly."

We Have Pictures

The agents who had lurked outside Norbert's house taking photographs stood stiffly in front of KGB Colonel Biroschnikov.

He said, "Hurry up. What have you got?"

"The shipyard worker went into Norbert's house."

Biroschnikov ordered, "Watch that house. Follow this unknown man from the dock and tell me where he goes."

The agent handed the colonel an envelope. "We have pictures." A roll of film from the envelope fell onto the desk.

Biroschnikov took the roll of film. "So what is this?"

"Pictures of the unknown man going into Norbert's house."

"Is the house a meeting place for union workers?"

"Yes, Comrade Colonel."

Biroschnikov handed the film to the chief of the local secret police. "Get this developed immediately."

The photos had been developed and printed by the time Colonel Biroschnikov returned the next day from breakfast with his agents. When he returned, he found the photographers waiting for him. After he studied the grainy black-and-white prints, he said, "Do any of you know who this stranger is?"

"No, Comrade Colonel," one of the photographers replied.

The colonel spread the photos on his desk. "They are very dark. I don't know if we can identify the man entering the house. However, you did very well. I'll see you get extra benefits." He motioned to the chief of the local secret police. "Take several men and bring Norbert here for questioning."

The chief of the local secret police asked, "What about General Prime Minister Jaruzelski's decree?"

"I'll deal with that worm. Moscow is now in charge if anyone wants to know."

Filip and Jacob moved invisibly through the dimly lit streets. Three tough-looking men stepped out of the shadows and followed the priest and his companion.

Filip told Jacob, "These guys following us. I'll take the goon on the right. You circle behind them and do what you can. Let's go."

As Filip and the priest dashed across the street, the three pursuers quickly followed. Jacob swung to one side and came up behind the three hostile men, while Filip confronted the man on the right side.

"You. Yeah, you right there," one of the assailants said. "We've got you now, traitor."

"What do you want, Comrades?" Filip questioned.

"The reward for taking you and your friend to the police."

Jacob said, "I don't think that is God's will at the moment, Comrades."

"We'll see about that," one of the men snapped back.

One of the attackers rushed Filip with a large knife.

Filip kicked him in the knee, forcing him to fall.

Jacob had a stranglehold around the second man's neck as Filip attacked the third thug and knocked him unconscious. The man with the injured knee tried to reenter the fray, but Filip kicked him in the other knee. He looked over and saw that Jacob rendered the second man unconscious with his bare hands.

Filip grabbed Jacob's sleeve and pulled him as they rushed into the darkness.

He told the priest, "You should have killed him."

"Priests do not kill," Jacob noted.

"What if your life is in danger, and it's him or you?"

Jacob said, "That was not the case this time."

"What about next time?"

"We'll just have to see."

Lying Is a Sin

Police hustled Norbert into a drab, gray-colored interrogation room. It was devoid of any furniture except two chairs and a desk. Biroschnikov sat behind the desk. Before him was a pad and a pencil; off to his right arm was a telephone. High up on the wall were two windows that let in a dim light.

Two agents roughly sat the interrogator's visitor on a wooden straight-back chair under two bright lights. One of the agents slapped Norbert's face and shoved him to make him fall off the chair, but Norbert stayed seated. He knew the agent was roughing him up, tenderizing him for questioning. And then they left the room.

Biroschnikov asked, "Comrade Norbert. What do you do at the shipyard?"

"I am a foreman."

"You want to keep your job?"

"Of course."

Biroschnikov said, "Someone parachuted into Poland and went to the Gdansk area. We think he visited your house. Did he?"

"No," Norbert responded. "If I learn anything, I'll tell you."

The KGB agent asked, "You're Catholic, right?"

Norbert answered, "Why should that matter?"

"Then you know how serious it is for Catholics to tell lies. I understand it's called a sin."

"Depends, Comrade, whether you have a need to know."

The KGB officer hit Norbert with a heavy rubber truncheon. Biroschnikov sneered. "You think you're a smart guy? Tell me what happened at your house last night, and no more bullshit."

"My friends and I were just playing cards and drinking a little."

The Soviet officer asked, "Where did the stranger go?"

"I don't know about any stranger."

"You are lying, but we can make you tell me the truth." He picked up the photos from his desk and handed them to Norbert. "Look at these photos."

"What are these?" Norbert questioned.

"Who was that man at your door?"

Norbert answered calmly. "Alfons. He is another worker at the Lenin Shipyard."

Biroschnikov closely studied Norbert face. He said, "Are you sure this is Alfons in the photo?"

"Yes."

About that time, the chief of police entered the room. Biroschnikov turned to the chief and asked him, "Does this look like Alfons?"

The chief of the secret police studied the pictures and answered, "It is too dark to identify him."

The KGB officer asked Norbert, "Did you recently get a new worker at the Lenin Shipyard?"

"Not that I am aware of, Comrade."

"I'll have my men check that out, and if you are lying, you will suffer for it."

Norbert sat still and said, "I am sure there is no new worker at the shipyard."

Biroschnikov called in his guard and ordered, "Get this fool out of here. And, Norbert, I'll personally be watching you."

As the chief of the local secret police and the guard took Norbert out, another secret agent rushed into the office.

He breathlessly said, "Comrade Colonel, three of our men were beaten up tonight."

"Where?"

"In the Glowne Miasto. Near St. Nicholas Church."

The KGB officer turned to Norbert. "Hold it. That's not far from your house, right?"

"It's not really that close."

"Comrade Norbert, explain what happened."

Norbert told him he had nothing to do with the event. Biroschnikov took Norbert into another room. Seated were the three injured men, showing signs of being beaten.

Birey got hurt.

"We tried to arrest the stranger."

"You fools. You had the address. It should have been easy."

"We went to the house, but he slipped away with another man. We had to chase them."

The colonel shouted, "Idiots! Let me guess what happened. You were overcome by two men."

"I think the stranger is a priest," one of the men noted.

"What do you mean?"

"I heard the man with him call him Father."

Biroschnikov spoke to Norbert. "Is he working with the Solidarity bastards?"

Norbert shrugged his answer.

The secret policeman said, "I am not sure. If he is a priest, then he works with Solidarity."

The chief of the secret police added, "And the pope too."

Biroschnikov spat. "Little good that will do them."

The chief of police asked, "What if the priest is headed to East Germany?"

"Why would he go there?" Biroschnikov questioned.

"The East Berlin partisans help escapees get to the West."

"But the wall. Surely it will stop him."

"Not always. Not if he has help. Like the CIA and West German scum."

Biroschnikov asked, "What is the name of the stasi commander there?"

"Comrade Commander Holgar," the chief answered.

Biroschnikov called for his car and said, "Notify the airport. I leave for Berlin right now."

Before he could exit his office, a policeman holding a file folder rushed in. He said, "Comrade Colonel, I think you want to see this."

He said, "I am busy. Why bother me with this fucking file that is nearly thirty years old?"

"It's actually thirty-three years old, sir. Look at the document on page ten. It's your signature, correct?"

Can You Get Me into West Berlin?

Rolf, a member of the Polish underground, led Jacob down the Gdansk Nowy Port pier in the dark to a moored fishing trawler on the Kanal Portowy that went to the Zatoka Gdanska. He had survived the 1944 ghetto uprising by escaping to the forest where he joined the resistance. Jacob was dressed as a fishing boat deckhand with his visor cap and foul weather clothing. Rolf helped him step aboard the vessel and then vanished into the night.

The vessel was forty feet in length with the wheelhouse upfront and fishing nets neatly rolled in the back. Although Jacob was forbidden to travel to East Berlin for escape to the West, the partisans told him it was easier than going from Poland into a non-Communist country such as West Germany.

Jacob told himself, *I must stick to the pope's plan.* "I'm not sure that is a good plan," he said to Rolf. "The pope would not approve."

Rolf told him, "It's for your safety. The authorities will think you will be traveling a different route into Germany by automobile, and that's where they will be looking for you on the highways and back roads. And besides, the underground and the CIA can easily get you from East Berlin into West Berlin and from there to Italy."

Jacob often thought about what Karyn's life must be like under Communism; he wondered how he would help her escape if he had a chance. He felt regret and guilt, recalling how he let her go and went home to Michigan where he was free and safe. He wondered if he were now looking for redemption.

The captain motioned for Jacob to follow him into the wheelhouse where a deckhand named Wilfred was making coffee.

The captain was a man in his fifties. He looked tired but also appeared capable and confident in his abilities to carry out the mission he was about to explain to Jacob.

The three stood around the chart table, watching the captain point to the route the trawler would follow from Gdansk to the Baltic Sea then westward to where the boat would enter a bay and go south on the Oder River.

The captain told Jacob, "You will leave the boat and get into a car at Frankfurt on the Oder River in East Germany for the next leg of your seventy-eight-mile trip to East Berlin."

Filip had explained to him, "From Frankfurt, you will travel westward on the autobahn to Schonefelder Kreuz, where you will get into another car that will take you into East Berlin."

"How can you get me into West Berlin?" Jacob questioned.

"It's done many times. We bribe the guards with Western money, good scotch whiskey, and American cigarettes."

Jacob reminded him, "They kill people trying to escape."

When the captain saw through the wheelhouse window two Polish secret police agents approach the boat, he said, "We have visitors." He told Wilfred, "Take the priest below."

As Wilfred and Jacob disappeared, the wheelhouse door suddenly opened.

The agent demanded, "What's your business here, Comrade? Documents."

The captain handed his papers to the policeman and explained, "I am leaving for Wolin to catch fish."

Wilfred came into the wheelhouse. The agents checked his papers. "We are looking for a man who may try to escape by water."

The captain told them, "I'll watch for him, Comrade Officers."

"If you see him, call for your reward."

Wilfred asked, "Who is the man you look for?"

"He's an enemy of the state."

"Yes, we must keep our nation pure, Comrade Officers."

The agent said, "We search below. What's there?"

"Fishing nets and other gear."

One of the agents went below, looked around, returned, and handed papers back to the captain and Wilfred. The lead agent said, "Have a safe voyage. Catch plenty of fish."

"I do my best, Comrades."

"Looks like you have what it takes."

The captain said, "I've been at it a long time."

"You should have good fishing this time of year."

Ten minutes after the agents left the boat, the trawler slowly left the dock after Wilfred unhooked the lines. The captain told Wilfred to bring the priest topside. After Jacob was in the wheelhouse, the captain offered him a cup of fresh coffee."

At the end of the voyage to Frankfurt in East Germany, the captain eased back on the throttle and guided the boat slowly against the dock. Jacob and Wilfred tied boat lines to the dock cleats. They were met by border guards who carefully checked their forged documents before letting them enter East Germany. "We see nothing wrong," they said.

Jacob said, "I don't see anyone to greet us. Where are they?"

As the captain told him not to worry, two men came out of the shadows.

The first man was named Heinz. "Welcome, Father. I take you to the car for your trip to East Berlin. You're going home, Father—at last. First through the East Germany workers' paradise, as predicted by honorable Comrade Lenin." He spat onto the ground. "And then on to Rome."

Wilfred untied the trawler and got onboard. The captain revved the engines before slowly moving the craft away to disappear into darkness.

Heinz and his fellow partisan, Edmund, led Jacob into a thicket of trees. When they got close to the car, Edmund stopped Jacob and said, "looks like the police found the car and will be watching. We have to change plans and go on foot immediately."

They walked two miles through a forest of trees growing close enough to hide them from an observer. Heinz said, "We go to an underground safe spot that the partisans used during World War II."

Immediately after arriving, a member of the local group gave Heinz the keys to an old dark-green Mercedes.

After Heinz and Jacob were inside, a tall woman, Marlene, and a man named Helmut got in the back seat with Jacob. Heinz started the car and began the drive to East Berlin.

About the Woman in East Berlin

Jacob was soon asleep next to Marlene. She was a buxom blonde with hair down to her shoulders. Besides being six feet tall, she was muscular. She had high cheekbones and well-curved lips over her distinct chin. Jacob and Marlene traveled as a married couple.

Heinz drove deeper into East Germany. Heinz asked, "Who do you think told the police about the boat?"

Helmut answered that he would find out.

Jacob awakened and sleepily looked around, anxious at first and then relaxed when he recognized his companions. "Where are we?"

"We'll be in East Berlin in about forty-five minutes," Heinz told him.

Helmut asked, "Did you sleep okay?"

"I guess so."

Marlene said, "Father, you are too brave. You should not have come back. The secret police may soon find you. They always seem to find the one they hunt. The secret police have already killed a priest. The bastards have a long reach throughout the Communist bloc."

Heinz asked, "Father, are you sure you want to do this?"

Jacob told them, "I wonder at times like these if it was such a good idea, but there is a woman I promised to get out of East Berlin a long time ago, and if she is still there, I will do it this time."

Helmut asked, "How can you?"

Jacob replied, "The CIA will help."

Marlene said, "Isn't that romantic."

Heinz told her, "Hush up already. You are talking to a priest."

"I didn't know, and I was only teasing him." She smiled and said, "Then take me with you to your great America."

Jacob told her, "I would if only I could." Jacob, wanting to change the subject, asked, "How would the secret police know who I am?"

Heinz pointed out, "They may have a dossier on you because you once lived in Poland."

When Jacob told them it was too long ago, Marlene told him, "You don't know the long reach of the KGB."

"I thought I did."

"Not until you live with them."

Heinz added, "They have bottles with pieces of clothing of everyone."

Marlene explained, "So they can prepare the bloodhound search dogs."

Helmut said, "Your parents' records probably are with the stasi in East Germany right now."

"They don't throw anything away, Father," Marlene noted.

Heinz agreed. "The Russians have done this sort of thing for hundreds of years, and they showed the East Germany secret police how to do it."

Jacob asked, "Does it really work?"

Heinz told him, "Of course."

The drive continued in silence until Marlene said, "Now, Father, tell us about the *femme fatale* in East Berlin."

Jacob laughed and said she was just a good friend.

"How do you know this woman?"

"We met long ago. Before I became a priest."

Marlene asked, "Did she jilt you, Father?"

Jacob said, "Let's drop the subject. Okay? It was a very long time ago."

His companions chuckled. Marlene said, "As you say, babbo."

As soon as Heinz saw the roadblock ahead, he told the group, "Let me do the talking. Have your papers ready, and stay calm and relaxed." He stopped the car four feet from the East Germany barrier. A guard walked up to Heinz's window and looked inside.

Marlene handed him all the papers for the passengers. The guard silently looked through the documents and ordered everyone from the car.

The the group stepped from the car and stood in a group while a guard searched inside the car. Three other guards stood close, leering at Marlene, making kissing noises, and laughing like naughty little boys.

One of them asked, "Do you party?"

No one in the quartet spoke as the guard backed out from the car and handed the papers back to Helmut.

The guard gruffly told him, "That will be twenty West deutsche marks." Heinz smiled as he pulled out his wallet and removed the money.

A second guard walked up and asked Helmut, "Comrade, what are you doing with Western money?"

"I brought it for you."

The first guard said, "We should shoot you for breaking the law."

The second guard said, "We have here a savvy traveler."

Heinz told them, "I will be coming back this way. I'll bring you more."

The first guard told him, "Wait, the other guard also needs twenty." Heinz paid the extortion. The guards laughed and turned away toward their post. One of the guards gave a signal, and the barrier rose to let the car pass.

Later that day Jacob was in a group having a meal with four other men in Helmut's East Berlin apartment.

Jacob asked, "How will I get into West Berlin?"

Helmut answered, "The morning after tomorrow we place you into a truck gasoline tank that has been altered to hide you. Then the driver will take you across the border at Checkpoint Charlie and go three blocks to a garage where you will get out."

Jacob asked, "How will I get to Rome?"

"You might go by American military train in a corridor through East Berlin to the border station with West Germany in the south and then into Italy."

Is This Priest Polish?

Karyn Dietrich and her husband, Adolph, had just finished breakfast when there was a quiet knock on their apartment door. Adolf opened the door to face Werner Seitz.

Seitz stepped into the apartment and waited until Adolf closed and locked the door. He said, "In two days we smuggle a priest to the West."

Karyn said, "A priest? What kind of priest?"

Seitz answered, "A priest who comes from Gdansk, Poland, and now must get back to Rome."

Adolf inquired, "Is this priest Polish? What's going on?"

Werner told him, "All I know is that he was born in Poland, but he is American on a mission for the Holy Father."

Adolf asked, "What's his name?"

"Jacob Gorska."

Karyn gasped and put her hands to her mouth. "My God."

Adolf saw that she was trembling. "What is it, liebling?"

Karyn rushed from the room.

Adolf walked into the bedroom and put his arms around Karyn. She was crying and sobbed, "He is the man I told you about—the one I met in Yugoslavia."

"The same who visited you here?"

She said, "Yes."

He told her, "Impossible."

"What if it's true?"

"Makes no difference," Adolf said. "We must get him into West Berlin."

Adolf and Karyn returned to the kitchen where Werner was waiting.

Adolf told him, "We may have a problem."

"What?"

"Karyn said she might know the priest."

"Makes no difference."

"That's what I told her."

Werner told them, "We have his escape all set." He turned to Karyn. "He won't know you're here, so don't worry."

Karyn cried into Adolf's shoulder. "The police will find him and kill him."

Two days later, Karyn knocked on the front door of a house in the outskirts of East Berlin. A member of the underground, Rolf, answered the door. He motioned for Karyn to step inside.

"I want to see the priest," she told him.

The Shield and the Sword

A large red-and-gold seal with raised images of a shield and a sword covered most of the wall behind Col. Holgar Braun's desk in the Department of State Security of the German (Communist) Democratic Republic, aka the stasi, housed in the former Berlin gestapo headquarters building. Holgar could best be described as a dandy who always wore freshly pressed uniforms, handmade shirts, and expensive silk ties. His height was six foot two, and his body was lean as a result of his diet and daily gym workout.

His office was like any other in the gray concrete buildings built by the Nazis and Soviets. The interior walls were painted a depressing gray, designed to convey to visitors and arrestees alike that it was hopeless to think one could deal successfully with the secret police.

This day he was angry, belligerent, menacing, overbearing, and dominating the men at his daily briefing meeting. He banged his hand hard on the table. It shook the room and caused the attendees to flinch.

With the combined intelligence of the KGB and the Polish secret police, it had been decided that the foreign invader was a priest from the United States. Moscow became quite concerned upon learning of this. Leaders of the USSR in their paranoia felt threatened whenever there was any action taking place in any of the client states like Poland, so they immediately set about investigating.

Holgar shouted, "Moscow and Warsaw want to know how you idiots let that fucking priest get into the DDR and not get arrested."

The five men around the table remained silent. Holgar grumbled. "He wasn't stopped in Poland. So now it is our job."

A plain-clothed agent rushed into the room

"Can't you see we're busy?" Holgar snapped. "What do you want so urgently, Martin?"

"The priest is here in East Berlin."

Holgar threw a crystal ashtray across the room at the wall where it was converted into shards of glass. He shouted, "I knew this would happen. Find and kill the fucking priest." He glared at the men seated around the table. "If he gets away, you are all dead. Don't just sit there; get off your asses and find him." Holgar banged his hand hard on the table.

A second soldier rushed into the office. "There's a phone call for you."

"Who's calling? Can't you see I'm busy?"

"Comrade Mielke."

Col. Gen. Erich Mielke was the commander of stasi, the state security system of secret police. Like the heads of all Communist regimes, the DDR dictators could not have existed without their secret police. This was the stasi.

A ministry for state security was an idea originated by Lenin in theory and developed by Stalin in practice, in both cases ostensibly for the defense of the 1917 Russian Revolution.

When the Second World War ended, Erich Mielke became the Soviet Union's man in Germany and supervised the creation of the DDR stasi organization. It was a combination of the Nazi gestapo and the Mafia. Before that, the NKVD was the Soviet secret police organization that surreptitiously moved into Poland notwithstanding Stalin's agreement that he would allow the country to be free and independent.

In December 1981 the stasi's domestic counterintelligence operation group was established in Warsaw, requested by the Kremlin's KGB chairman Yuri Andropov and Poland's Communist Party chief Erich Honecker, who was watching the growth of Solidarity. As it turned out, the restiveness of the Polish workers signaled what the Kremlin Communists feared: the downfall of Polish Communism.

The fear was that the Polish germ, so to speak, could spread to East Germany, and thus, the stasi of the East German Communist regime was established in Poland. In addition to the stasi's domestic counterintelligence department, Mielke ordered Gen. Markus Wolf to form a foreign espionage department.

Wolf had been raised and influenced by parents who were members of the German Communist Party. After the war, Wolf was first trained in Moscow to be a diplomat, and in 1952 he joined the stasi to become one of, if not *the*, greatest spymaster.

The domestic counterintelligence and foreignespionage departments worked with the Polish secret police. Stasi agents were assigned to East German consulates throughout Poland. Networks were established to shadow church and labor leaders, provide photographs and videotapes, and carry out bugging telephones in various government offices. Informants were lured and recruited from the military and rewarded with extra food rations and luxuries that were denied to the average Pole. Included were Western cigarettes and other scarce items, such as soap. Later informants were rewarded with medals and money.

Holgar knew of this history, as well as DDR intelligence, and so he cautiously decided to take the phone and talk to Mielke. Holgar told his group to leave the room.

He heard Mielke shout into the phone, "Moscow wants to know what you idiots are doing to capture the priest."

"I just learned he was here."

"Why didn't you know that before now?"

Holgar told him, "We are right on it, Comrade."

"It's your neck."

Holgar assured Mielke that he was aware of that before he hung up and threw the phone against the wall. He called for Martin and told him, "You are in charge of this operation, and you better not fail. If you fail, you are history."

"Yes, Comrade."

After seeing the turmoil in Poland, President Reagan had decided he would use it to bury the Communist system, and so ordered CIA Director Casey to provide secret support to solidarity, which included printing and other communications equipment. The Polish Pope John Paul II and his church officials with contacts in Poland were to act as conduits for money and equipment to Solidarity. By 1982 the Polish underground activities intensified with the result that all communications traffic, including mail in and out of Poland, was put under stasi control. Approximately thirty-four thousand Poles worked in East German industry. Eventually, the political climate and antigovernment opposition groups grew in other Eastern European countries, along with that of the DDR.

I Didn't Abandon You

Karyn asked where the priest was.

Rolf said, "What priest?"

"The one Werner told me about."

Rolf flared with anger. "Where did Werner tell you this?"

"He came to our apartment."

Rolf stamped his foot. "Shit. He is a fool. Your home is bugged."

Karyn again asked about the priest. Rolf pointed to the floor above. He told her, "I have to go out and see how to move him now." He grabbed a jacket from the hall rack. "Stay here until I get back."

Karyn nodded and went up the stairs.

Jacob was seated at a table writing and drinking vodka when he heard her knock on the door. When he opened the door, Karyn said, "Hello, Jacob."

He stood paralyzed.

She smiled at him. "May I come in, Father?"

Jacob said, "I'm not sure."

Karyn entered, forcing Jacob to step aside, far enough to ensure he did not touch her, as if she were diseased.

As he closed the door, she told him, "You don't look like a priest."

"You think I want to get shot?"

"It is so good to see you again, Jacob."

"Is it?" he asked.

She said, "Adolf told me you were in town."

"Who's Adolf?"

"My husband. He is helping you escape."

Karyn took his hand in hers. As Jacob pulled it away, he said, "Don't. Please."

She said, "I waited so long for you, Jacob, but you never came to get me. And you stopped writing to me. What happened to you?"

Karyn stepped closer. Jacob moved backward.

He answered, "Our governments could not work it out. Your stepfather is a Nazi war criminal. You should have told me."

"I didn't think it mattered."

"What? Me trying to get a Nazi war criminal relative out of East Germany? What were you thinking? That I was stupid?"

Karyn sat in a chair and began to cry. "I thought I would never see you again. You abandoned me. Why?"

"I didn't abandon you," Jacob told her. "It was impossible to get you to the West."

"You could have come and lived in Berlin."

"I don't think that would have been a solution." She said, "I am glad we are meeting like this."

"A lot has happened since those days in Berlin. We should not meet like this, Karyn."

"It is safe here for now."

"I mean, I am a priest," Jacob reminded her.

"You think I am temptation?"

"It's possible."

"Surely you're not in love with me anymore, Jacob. What could happen?"

Jacob stepped back from her and went to his desk to pick up his glass of vodka. He took a long drink before turning back toward her. "I didn't abandon you. I tried the impossible and failed."

Wiping tears from her face and standing up, she asked, "Why are you upset with me?" She walked close to him, face-to-face.

Jacob put his arms around her. "I'm sorry. I shouldn't be mean to you."

She relaxed and let her arms fall to her sides. "Why did you become a priest?"

"This is my vocation. And my mission now is my destiny."

"What do you mean?" Karyn asked.

"What I am doing helps the Polish people gain their freedom, and it gives me meaning to my life. It's the reason I became a priest."

She asked, "Why are you here?"

"I cannot tell you about that. What I can tell you is that I want to get you to the West."

"I am married now, and I have a son."

He answered, "Maybe there is a way to get all of you out of here."

"It's so dangerous to leave East Berlin. Aren't you afraid what can happen?"

"There must be a way," Jacob told her. "Others have made it."

They sat in chairs facing each other. She asked, "What do you mean by giving your life a meaning? You just live."

He asked, "Doesn't your life have meaning?"

"I once thought it did. When we planned to live life together. It's what I wanted—to spend the rest of my life with you. But you changed all that."

"Sometimes we have nothing to say about how our lives turn out," Jacob noted.

"Tell me about it," Karyn agreed.

"Do you live without purpose? Your life has no meaning?"

"You think too much, Jacob. You always like to find answers. Life is not as complicated as you make it."

He asked, "What do you mean?"

"You're born, you live, and then you die," she explained.

"What happens after death?"

She said, "Nothing."

"You really believe there's no afterlife?"

"Prove it exists."

"I can't. I believe. That's called faith."

"What if you are wrong?"

"If I am wrong, then Jesus was wrong. And if he was wrong and I live as if he were right, what difference will it make after I die?"

"That's my point. It will mean nothing."

He said, "But just suppose I am right—that I agree with Jesus."

"But you don't know for sure you are right."

"So what? What do I lose by living as if Jesus is right and what you believe and say is wrong?"

"Nothing except a different life."

"Exactly. If you were a gambling person, you would have to bet on my view. You can't lose. It's a matter of personal choice."

She said, "You would have spent your entire life believing in something that does not exist."

He smiled. "So? What have I lost in the end if I live as I believe and am wrong?"

"If that's the meaning of life, then I guess I live my life without meaning," she noted.

He said, "Yes. And is that what you want?"

"It's what we're taught."

"Just think about it. If you are wrong and I am right that God exists and we can see Him again after death, where will that leave you?"

"Will it really matter?"

"Yes."

She asked, "How?"

"If people live as if there is no God, why should they be good people? Why not live any way anyone sees fit? What keeps people from doing bad things?"

"You are saying that people who don't believe in God are bad?" He answered, "No. But what influences their moral compass?"

"We follow the laws."

"The laws of your country? Or the laws of God?"

"If we break the law, we are arrested and maybe sentenced to prison."

"Why don't you just move to the West?"

"There's the wall. I can't walk through a checkpoint and go to the West."

"Exactly," Jacob said. "To climb over that wall is a crime, right?"

"Of course."

"Is that a good law?"

"Of course."

"Why are your countrymen who want to go to the West prevented? Some are killed trying. Do you remember when you could walk to West Berlin, and no one stopped you?"

She shouted, "Of course I remember."

"So why call the law good if it imprisons you?"

She spoke with increasing anger. "The government said it is for our own good—to keep people like you from coming here."

"Me? What's so bad about me?"

"You want to corrupt our minds with lies from the West about how good you have it there."

"You don't remember what it was like?"

"What do you mean?" she asked.

He answered, "You and your friends used to work in the West and live in the East. The money you earned in the Western sector is worth more than East German marks. There were many of you. So why did the government stop you from working in the West and living here?"

"Too many of us were staying in the West."

"Ah-ha. Yes. And why did they want to do that?"

"I didn't want to do that."

"You told me in Yugoslavia that you would move, but your mother wanted to stay here."

"I wasn't going to leave my mother all alone. Why move? Life was good here."

"Was it? Or was it that you had the best of both worlds?" Jacob probed. "You earned Western marks. You lived like a princess in the East cheaply on money earned in the West."

"That was good."

He sensed the sarcasm. "Good? Then why did they build the wall? I remember I was staying with you when they put up the barbed wire."

"It was in the middle of the night," Karyn remembered aloud.

"Why such an odd hour?"

"I guess because there was less traffic."

He reminded her, "Maybe they did it when no one was looking, like thieves in the night."

"You sound just like Adolf," Karyn noted.

"I'd like to meet him," Jacob told her.

She said, "I am afraid he's going to get killed one of these days talking like he does and helping people go to the West."

"Has he ever offered to get you to the West?"

"I told him I can't leave mother, and she won't go."

Jacob said, "He's disobeying the law."

"Yes. You have to agree that one must obey the law."

"But who's law? Man's or God's? Is it a good law?"

"There is no God, so it must be man's law." Karyn turned toward the door when she heard the sound of a door banging shut downstairs. She walked away from Jacob.

There was a knock on the door. Jacob asked, "Who is it?"

"Rolf."

Rolf saw Karyn wiping her eyes and then he looked at Jacob.

Jacob said, "Karyn and I are old friends."

Rolf shrugged and told them, "We have to hurry you out of here."

Jacob grabbed his bag, which he'd already packed for the journey. He and Rolf rushed from the room, leaving a bewildered Karyn by herself and wondering what was next for her.

The Stasi Arrested Karyn and Henry

Rolf rushed into Jacob's room in CIA's East Berlin safe house and said, "They picked up Karyn and Henry."

"Who is Henry?" asked the priest.

"He's an agent with the CIA trying to keep Karyn from escaping." Jon, Karyn's son, asked, "What happened?"

Rolf explained how Karyn ran with Henry on a street near the wall on the East Berlin side. Two stasi cars raced around a corner and trapped them. Men jumped from both cars, grabbed Henry and Karyn, and forced them into the car.

"When they discovered that Henry was a CIA agent they killed him."

"Where is my father now?" Jon asked.

Rolf answered that he did not know but he was in danger for helping the escapees.

"Maybe he's already dead," said Jon.

Jacob hugged Jon and let him cry for his father.

At about that time a stasi agent escorted Karyn into Holgar's office where he was meeting with Biroschnikov. When Holgar confronted Karyn, she was scared but fought to hide it. Holgar told her she appeared frail. When Karyn asked Holgar what was happening, he smiled.

"Do you know who I am?" Holgar asked her.

"Of course," Karyn noted. "You're the chief pervert of perverts."

"I like your spirit. How is little Jon?"

Karyn became frightened. "Why do you ask?"

Holgar lit a cigarette. "It's nothing to worry about. I'm only curious about his welfare. We in the DDR want the best for our children."

"By whose standards?"

"Tsk, tsk, tsk, little *liebling*. Now that you are a widow, I am concerned."

A chill ran down her spine when she answered. "I am not a widow."

"Oh, yes you are." He opened a folder and read the top page. "As of two o'clock this morning, you have been a widow."

"Have you killed Adolf?"

Biroschnikov told her, "My men had to. He was forcing some of our patriotic people to leave East Germany. There was a gun battle. We built the wall to keep the capitalistic pigs out of our country. Your Adolf committed treason by forcing innocent people to become slaves of the West."

Karyn stepped forward and spit in Holgar's face.

He wiped off the spittle and shouted, "I can have you shot for that, but I won't. I have a request of you."

"You mean an order."

"Call it what you wish. Now that Adolf is dead, I want you and your son to live with me so he will have a good upbringing by a real man."

Karyn scoffed. "You'll have to kill me first."

"Sorry, I can't do that. I made a promise, and I am a man of my word. In time you will marry my assistant. He covets your lovely body."

"I am not a trophy for your thugs."

Holgar told Karyn, "I want you to meet Comrade Colonel Biroschnikov of the KGB, all the way from Moscow. He will see that you are arrested."

"You have no right to arrest me."

"Oh, yes we do. Your late husband was a traitor." Biroschnikov answered, "And you are part of the scheme to help escapees."

Karyn retorted, "I don't know what you're talking about."

Holgar said, "We think you and your dead husband were helping the priest."

"What priest?"

Biroschnikov scoffed. "You don't know about the American priest who is in East Berlin?"

"No, I don't."

Biroschnikov asked Holgar, "What are you going to do with this woman and her son?"

Holgar told him, "I can take care of them."

Karyn spat, "I wouldn't let you take care of my cat."

Biroschnikov offered Karyn a cigarette that she refused and angrily told him, "The only thing that I want is your head on the Berlin Wall."

Holgar told her, "The Honecker government is very upset with anyone aiding escapees."

"If people want to leave, why can't they?" she asked.

Biroschnikov explained, "Those who want to leave are allowed to leave. You are misguided and misinformed. They don't know how terrible it is in the capitalist society on the other side of the wall until they spend some time there."

Holgar again asked, "How is little Jon?"

Biroschnikov told him, "Not now, Comrade."

"I am only trying to help."

Biroschnikov said, "I know how you help boys."

Karyn said, "You'll pay for your atrocities."

"You should talk. We know all about your father and his crimes as a sadistic Nazi at Birkenau. We will not imprison you if you cooperate."

The KGB officer promised, "If you tell us where the priest hides, I will see you and Jon are well taken care of."

"I know of no priest," Karyn insisted.

Holgar laughed. "If your priest lover dies, to whom can you turn?" He then pushed a button on his desk. The door opened, and his agent, Franz, entered. "Lock this woman in the prison. Find her son, Jon, and take the boy to my house."

Franz grabbed Karyn. She struggled and shouted, "Jon did nothing wrong. Punish me, not him."

"I am not going to punish either of you. You will each have a good life," Holgar told her. "You are a fool not to accept my offer. What do you have for the boy? Nothing. I can give him everything."

She spoke defiantly. "You can't take my son away from me, Colonel."

"Yes I can, and I will. Now tell me where he is, or you go back to prison, and I'll find Jon anyway. Is that what you want?"

"I'll never surrender my son to you, because you are a pervert."

Holgar got close to her face. "What did you call me, bitch?"

"I called you a pervert."

He slapped Karyn's face twice and pushed her against a chair where she fell backward into it. He stood over her.

She shouted, "Take me. You can do anything you want with me, but leave Jon alone." She had heard that he didn't care for women so much as he did for young boys.

He spat on her. "You're not worth it, bitch."

She glared at him. "You don't like women, do you? You molest boys. You want my son for sex. That's it, isn't it? I'll tell everyone what you are doing to little boys."

"We have ways to make you talk."

Biroschnikov said, "Shut up, Comrade. I am in charge now. Perhaps she doesn't know where he is now." He turned to Karyn. "Just tell me if the priest has escaped."

"How should I know if I don't know of any priest?"

"Would you prefer to go to prison?" Biroschnikov asked.

"I don't care what you do, but leave my son alone."

Holgar told Franz, "Find this woman the worst cell in the prison."

Biroschnikov smiled and told her, "We'll find Jon."

Karyn shouted, "No. Please don't harm him. Jon has done nothing wrong. Punish me, not him."

Franz forcefully took Karyn from the room. He asked, "What about the young boy at your house?"

Holgar said, "Take him out and shoot him. He's of no use to me now."

Once they were alone, Biroschnikov said, "Well, Holgar, you certainly fucked that up. I almost had her talking." Then he walked out the door.

The Priest May Have Already Fled Poland

KGB Agent Biroschnikov had taken the folder from the policeman just as he was leaving Warsaw. After boarding the KGB plane for Gdansk, he opened it and more slowly read the top paper as he recalled his initial reaction. When Biroschnikov had flipped the pages, he exclaimed, "What the hell is this?"

The policeman pointed to the page and told him, "It deals with the man you hunt. It's a report on his parents."

"How do you know this?"

"An informer close to the partisans overheard a priest was dropped into Poland and went to the Gdansk area."

"What?"

"The partisans were talking about a man named Jacob Gorska. And I checked our files on Polish names."

Biroschnikov asked, "You mean the stranger in Gdansk is this priest?"

"Yes, Comrade. The man we hunt is their son. According to the file, this boy—now a priest—went to America in 1949."

"How do we know that?"

"Our agents in America have a file on the priest."

"I remember this boy. I executed his parents. They were Nazi collaborators. Why is the priest here?"

"It has to be something for Solidarity and the pope," the policeman noted.

"Or he's here to get revenge," Biroschnikov shouted. "We have to find this priest and kill him. If he lives, he can identify me as the killer of his parents, and because Stalin is dead, I have no one who can exonerate me."

"Do you really think the boy witnessed his parents' execution?"

"I am not sure, and I don't want to take chances."

"One good thing is that information is not in the file. But do you think he can still identify you?"

"With this mark?" He pointed to the purple coloration on his face.

"But it's been thirty years."

Biroschnikov promised, "I must silence him."

"But how did he escape Poland if the Russians were in control?"

"How the hell would I know?" Biroschnikov closed the file.

"Should I notify Comrade Commander Mielke in East Berlin in case the priest is there?"

After they arrived at Holgar's office, Biroschnikov said, "No. Get out and search the roads. Set up roadblocks."

"Yes, Comrade. But I think he may already have left Poland."

Biroschnikov banged his hand on the desk and shouted, "Find the fucking priest and kill him." He then commaned he speak with Holgar.

The agent in the office said, "The colonel is not here."

"Listen, dolt. I am Comrade Colonel Biroschnikov of the KGB. Where is he?"

"I am not sure, Comrade. I'll give him your message."

Biroschnikov snarled. "I don't leave messages. I must talk with him."

At the instant he was wanted by Biroschnikov, Holgar was in bed with an eleven-year-old boy who had just given him felacio. Holgar rolled the boy over onto his stomach and prepared to enter him from behind as he lubricated himself.

There was a loud banging on the door.

"Open up, Comrade Braun."

"Who is it?"

"Comrade Gen. Erich Mielke, minister of state security."

Holgar stepped naked from bed and put on a robe before he walked to the door and opened it slightly.

Mielke, seeing the bulge in Holgar's attire, smiled and asked with a smirk, "Am I disturbing anything?"

"What is it you want?"

Mielke pushed the door open and walked past Holgar, who protested. The naked young boy grabbed his clothes and jumped up.

Mielke snapped, "I don't explain my actions. What is happening here?"

"It is not like it seems."

"Send your boy out of the room."

The naked boy disappeared through the bathroom door.

Holgar said, "I can explain everything."

"Comrade Holgar, we have a bigger problem than where you put your prick. An American priest left Poland, and we have intelligence he heads this way."

Holgar noted that he was already hunting for him.

"What do you mean?" Mielke questioned.

"Warsaw called East Germany leader Erich Honecker."

"I guess you don't spend all your time in bed with young boys."

"I do not, Comrade. I shall find and kill the priest."

Mielke ordered, "Report only to me. But you will kill the fucking priest, or we kill you, Comrade Holgar. I will personally slice your penis from your body, stick it in your mouth, and leave you to bleed to death." He turned to leave.

Holgar said proudly, "You can count on me."

Mielke shouted, "In the name Lenin, get rid of that boy bitch."

Once They Were Lovers

Vatican City, Rome, is the State of the Vatican—an area of 110 acres and a population of an estimated one thousand people, thus making it the smallest state in the world. It is ruled by the Bishop of Rome, the pope.

The Vatican Palace, built as the pope's residence, is located just north of St. Peter's Basilica. The building contains the Papal Apartments, including the official residence of the pope and various offices of the Catholic Church, as well the Vatican Library.

It was in one of these offices that Vatican secretary of state Cardinal Casaroli met with US national security adviser Richard Allen. The cardinal motioned Allen to the chair next to his.

He told Allen, "I have information that Father Gorska wants to bring a woman and her son out of East Berlin." The cardinal added, "This would be intolerable."

Allen asked, "What's he doing in East Berlin? That is not part of his mission, is it?"

"No."

Allen said, "You must somehow get word to Father Gorska to abandon his plan."

The cardinal asked, "Are you somehow able to do it?"

"Of course. We should be able to do that. Who is this woman?"

"Her name is Karyn. She and Father Gorska were once lovers in East Berlin."

Allen asked, "As a priest?"

"No. when he was in college in the nineteen sixties."

It was Allen who asked, "So why is he so eager to get this woman out of East Germany?"

Casaroli opened a file in front of him before answering. "I am not sure, but we think he's trying to correct a problem from their past."

Allen told him, "He may be seeking redemption, but what he wants is certainly not our business, nor that of the CIA. Look at how it will be perceived after the media do what they do to sensationalize news of a priest and a woman escaping East Berlin together."

"Just so I understand," the cardinal cautiously began. "You and I have an agreement to keep the priest from going into East Berlin. My fear is that he will be caught and possibly killed in his attempt."

Allen and the cardinal shook hands to seal the agreement.

Don't Even Think about It

Jacob, Adolf, and Marlene talked with CIA agent Bill Casey inside a safe house in East Berlin.

Bill told the group, "If this meeting is about using the CIA to get Karyn and her son into the West, don't even think about it."

Jacob answered, "I won't go without Karyn."

"You may have nothing to say about it. The pope and President Reagan do not want you to make the trip and possibly start an international incident."

Jacob said, "I've heard that before."

Adolf said, "Reagan is just like President Kennedy in the sixties who wouldn't test the Reds. The city should never have been divided."

Bill told him, "I can agree. But Father Gorska is under orders to get back to Rome according to the pope's plan as quickly as possible. That's what we signed on for. Nothing more."

Jacob said, "Rome does not understand the situation."

"It's too hot politically to get an East Berliner out at this time."

Marlene asked, "And exactly what is your plan for Father Gorska?"

Bill told her, "False passport and necessary papers to pass through Checkpoint Charlie in a military or possibly a diplomatic licensed vehicle."

"You think they won't recognize him?"

Bill answered, "We have that covered. Don't worry."

Marlene was warning him to not to be so sure when Jacob interrupted. "Sorry, no deal. Karyn comes, or I stay."

Bill told him, "East Berlin and West Berlin are working on a treaty agreement to ease visits from East to West. Your foolishness can destroy all that."

Marlene scoffed. "Such visits will never happen."

Bill informed them, "President Honecker has his orders from Moscow. The Kremlin wants him to peacefully resolve all issues and not pull the Kremlin into it."

"It's a trick by the Reds to keep control."

Bill asked, "Father, do you really want to disobey the Holy Father and the superior general of the Jesuits?"

Jacob told him, "Once Rome realizes what we're dealing with here, I will get permission."

Bill replied, "Maybe Rome will agree. But not the CIA."

"We'll just have to negotiate, won't we?"

Bill told him, "The pope told us in no uncertain terms that he would not permit you to bring anyone out with you."

Marlene said, "It's the Prague Spring all over again."

What she referred to had been August 20, 1968, when the Soviets invaded Czechoslovakia by a few armored vehicles, and only a small group of high-ranking Soviet officers and officials knew that it was only the beginning of a full-scale invasion of Czechoslovakia. She added, "It was a dictatorship attacking a democracy to impose its will on another country."

Bill stood up to signal the meeting was over. "I can't play this game, so I am leaving. What happens is up to you. So goodbye and good luck." He promptly left the house.

Marlene said, "Well, Padre, the ball is in your court."

Adolf added, "And you're the only one who can play."

Shortly thereafter, the group left the safe house.

Kill Father Jacob on Sight

Five men and one woman sat in a semicircle in front of a desk in the Berlin Operations Station of the CIA, aka the BOB. The man behind the desk was station chief Brad Murphy.

He asked, "Where's the priest now?"

"Our men have him in a safe house in East Berlin," one of the men reported.

Murphy asked about the rest of Jacob's group.

"Adolf was shot dead in East Berlin trying to run for it when police discovered he was in the process of helping the escapees. Rolf is with the priest, and Karyn is still at large."

Next, Murphy asked about Holgar.

"He has ordered his men to kill Father Jacob on sight."

"Well, we can't let that happen. Director Casey will have our heads if anything happens to the priest."

The group nodded as a unit.

Murphy asked about the scuba gear for Jacob to use while swimming across the Spree River underwater.

"We have the equipment on the way to the safe house."

Two CIA men entered the CIA East Berlin safe house where Jacob and Rolf sat at a table eating a late supper of bread, cheese, wine, and bratwurst with sauerkraut. The men set down two sets of underwater scuba diving gear.

Rolf said, "Looks like we swim to freedom, Father."

The priest walked over to the gear, checked it, and discovered a faulty air hose. "This has to be replaced."

One of the visitors, Mike, took some spare parts from a large bag and made the repair. The other man, Curt, unfolded a map of Berlin on the table and traced a black line from point A to point B on the Spree River where the escape would take place. "In two hours, we take you to this point. You enter the Spree on the eastern side and swim underwater to the western side. Army soldiers will be waiting for you," he explained.

Jacob asked, "Can the East Germans shoot at us as we exit the water?"

Mike said, "No. It is a firm policy not to shoot anyone on Western soil. But they will shoot at you in the water if they spot you. So you have to swim more than three feet deep, because the bullets will not be deadly at that depth."

Rolf asked about air bubbles from breathing and showed in the water where they would be.

Jon explained, "We have given you rebreather equipment, which captures your exhaled air and removes the CO_2 from the air that you will then again breathe."

Jacob said, "This is all well and good for me, but what about Karyn and her son?"

Mike answered, "We have it arranged to smuggle Karyn and her son through Checkpoint Charlie into the American sector."

Who Let Her Escape?

Holgar had taken a telephone call from Mielke, the chief of state security, who told him, " Jacob plans to go over the wall to the West."

"I didn't know that," whispered Holgar timidly.

The chief shouted, "Of course you didn't know this, idiot. You have been wasting time lying around with young boys. You are more useless than tits on a boar."

Holgar flinched when he heard the loud noise made by his caller slamming down his phone.

The next day, after his agents searched for Jon without success, Holgar called the jail. "Let the woman go."

"She is not here, Comrade."

Holgar shouted, "You idiot. She has to be there. Where could she have gone?"

"I'm sorry, Comrade, but she was never brought in," the guard explained.

Holgar banged down the telephone. He thought he knew what had happened. He muttered to himself. "It was Franz who let her escape."

Because he had a meeting scheduled, he would have to deal with Franz later. At the prescheduled time, Holgar watched his top agents file silently into his office, take their seats, and watch as Holgar paced his office in front of them. In the corner sat a frightened boy.

Holgar ordered, "Frederick, you take three men to the home of this traitor Norbert. Josef, take the others to Rolf's home and get the priest if he's there. Bring him here for interrogation. And then we will kill him."

"What about Karyn?"

"I'll take care of that *cagna* (bitch) myself."

Holgar screamed at his agents, "You fools. Mielke said you must not let the priest go over the wall."

An agent, Manfred, said under his breath, "Is this guy a wonder priest?"

Josef asked Holgar, "How do you know this is true?"

"The chief of state security called me with this news. You satisfied now?"

Frederick offered, "He may already be in Italy."

Manfred promised, "Sir, I can put my best men in Italy to kill this priest."

Holgar shot back, "You said that about the agents who are now dead."

"But now we know more about this priest."

"What the fuck are you talking about? You're all delusional." Holgar's shrill voice shook the room. "You were supposed to kill the fucking priest, idiots. He was helping Solidarity in Poland, and I now have the DDR chief of state security on my ass." He waved a dismissal.

The group was then disbanded and quickly exited Holgar's office.

Holgar murmured, "Shit. How do these things happened when we have the best secret police in the world?"

He felt better after the door closed. Holgar motioned for the boy in the corner to come to him. He reluctantly walked to Holgar, who said, "We have time for bed, darling. I need some release."

He led the boy into an adjacent room with a military cot he used for naps, and as he did so, he slowly stroked the boy's bare buttocks under his pants.

The Soviet Bloc Is Collapsing

Franz and Karyn walked by separate paths to East Berlin's Museum Island on the Spree River.

"I don't think we will be found here," he told her when they met.

Franz was secretly meeting with Karyn, whom he had not taken to the jail as Holgar ordered. They found a bench in the Basilica Room quiet area in the Pergamon Museum with its marvelous Oriental and Greco-Roman antiquities. He had told her that he decided to help her, Jon, and the priest escape in order to save himself. He verified intel from Warsaw and deduced that if he helped the group, the CIA would help him to escape also.

They were seated on the bench in front of the large oil painting by Marco della Robbia of the virgin mother, Christ child, and the saints. Franz told Karyn that Holgar's plan was to stop her group as they tried to escape, getting to the wall and over it.

She did not disclose the latest escape plans for Jacob, herself, and her son. Instead, she said, "You risk your life getting me out of jail and meeting me, Comrade."

"I can get you and Jon and the priest safely to West Berlin."

"Why would you do that?" Karyn asked.

Franz declared, "You think I want to die here? I have had enough of Holgar and his vicious, vulgar ways. I've had enough of the Soviets and the KGB, and the stasi are worse than the gestapo ever was."

"What you do for us?"

"I will set up the escape. Don't tell anyone. Stasi spies are everywhere," he warned.

"I must tell my group."

"You can, but be careful."

She said, "I promise. But you have to tell us your plan of escape."

"Yes."

Karyn told Franz, "Thank you for the help. I would not be here except for you."

He said, "There are changes taking place, and I want to be on the winning side. I see now that DDR conservatives will never let Germany be free."

She was suspicious. "You're trying to trick me into cooperating so your boss can kill the priest." She stared at Franz. "You're not serious."

"Yes I am," Franz assured her. "The Soviets want to kill your priest because he helps Poland gain freedom. I will be killed for what I now believe if Holgar reports me to the party bosses."

"And what is it you believe?" Karyn questioned.

"That the Soviet bloc is collapsing even as I speak," he answered.

She smiled. "So you can't beat the priest. That's why you want to help."

"If Poland gets its freedom, so can Germany. I want to be part of this change."

She laughed. "Because you are stasi, your days are numbered. I don't blame you for escaping."

"Set up the meeting and tell me when and where it is."

"I should be able to meet with my group tonight."

What about the Guards?

It was early morning inside a small cafe two miles from the center of East Berlin. Jacob sat with Otto and Alfons. Karyn had told them about her meeting with Franz.

Jacob asked, "How do we know he isn't setting a trap with the pig Holgar."

"We don't know for sure," Otto admitted.

Alfons said, "We have to be sure Franz is really helping us."

Jacob suggested, "He has to give us a sign—something for security."

Alfons said, "Don't trust Franz. You have your plan. Let him find his own way out."

Otto said, "Franz knows the zones where the no-man's-land is free of land mines."

"What's it for?" asked Jacob.

"In case the West invades East Germany, the Soviets can run their tanks defensively through the zone into the Western sectors."

Jacob smiled. "Or in case the East Germans decide to invade and conquer West Berlin." He quickly asked, "What about the guards and the searchlights? Who will kill them long enough to give us the time we will need to let us get over the wall unseen?"

Alfons suggested, "Otto you will have to resolve that out if Jacob is to get out alive."

Two big East German policemen entered the cafe, stopped, and looked around. They stared a long time at Jacob's group. One of the policemen walked over to the table. "Your documents. Now."

Jacob, Karyn, and Otto handed their papers to the officer who studied them, handed them back, and asked, "What are you doing here?"

In perfect German, Otto answered, "Planning the revolution."

The policemen laughed. "I'll bet. You should be in the West doing what Lenin did in Russia."

Alfons said, "Exactly what I was saying, but we cannot get to the West."

Jacob kicked Otto under the table. Otto's face went white.

The policeman asked, "Are you the priest we are looking for?"

Jacob told him, "Do I look like a priest? If you need a priest, I can look for one, though."

The policemen laughed. "Buy me and my friend some schnapps before I arrest all of you."

Otto waved to the waiter. "Drinks for my friends, please. Whatever they want."

The policeman said, "I was only joking."

"You deserve a drink, Officer. You have a nasty job."

"For sure. I hope I don't have to shoot a friend trying to escape to the West."

After they emptied their glasses, the policemen waved as they left.

Jacob asked Otto, "Are you trying to get us killed?"

He laughed. "I think it all went very well."

The Gas Tank Escape

In an East Berlin neighborhood, Karyn, Jon, and Rolf entered a garage where Heinrich, a member of the resistance, was removing the metal top of a gasoline tank on the side of a truck. The tank was large enough to conceal Karyn.

Heinrich Greiss was an experienced underground teenage fighter who was part of a sabotage group in the spring of 1945 whose major job was causing as much damage as possible to the railway lines used by the German government to ship fuel, food, and weapons to the armies retreating from Allied forces marching north through Italy in their attempt to push the German military back to Berlin. After the building of the Berlin wall in 1961 he joined East Berliners dedicated to helping the escapees to West Berlin.

Rolf explained to her that she would be the first to go across the border.

She asked, "What about Jon?"

"He goes the next trip."

Heinrich helped Karyn into the bottom of the tank.

Karyn asked him, "What about the priest?"

"I have heard nothing new," Rolf admitted.

Heinrich told her, "The CIA is taking care of his escape."

"The priest had to go separately. It was Vatican and CIA orders."

Karyn curled up into a ball so Rolf could attach the metal plate covering her. Over that, he attached the top of the tank, which had been modified so that he could fill it with gasoline.

He tightly wrenched the bolts holding the tank sections together. When done, Hans knocked on the tank. "Can you hear me?"

"Yes," she answered.

"In thirty minutes you'll be in West Berlin and free. I'll drive you."

Hans poured gasoline into the top of the tank so that it looked like the entire tank was full of fuel and then got behind the wheel. He pulled out of the garage and headed for Checkpoint Charlie. The truck would first have to stop on the East German side for inspection.

An East Berlin border guard walked to the truck and ordered Hans out. He stepped from the cab. A guard held a pole with a mirror on the end that he placed beneath the truck and looked for contraband as he moved the mirror from the front to the rear.

Another guard stepped up and looked inside the truck's cabin and then stepped down. "Papers," he demanded. While he looked at them, he said, "You are smuggling people across the border, no?"

Hans said, "Of course not, Comrade Officer. If I get the chance, I smuggle them back here."

"That I want to see." He closely looked at Hans's face, looked at the photo on the papers, and again looked at Hans. He did this several times before he said, "This picture does not look like you."

"It's me."

"Are these forged documents?"

Hans pointed. "Look at the stasi stamp."

"What's the purpose of your entry into the American sector?"

"I'm picking up a load for the Soviet Army headquarters," Hans lied.

"What are you picking up?"

"I don't know. My orders are just to make the pickup."

"Probably American cigarettes and chocolates. I could use some of both."

The other guard joined him. "Or malt scotch for the working class."

The first guard walked to the rear of the truck. "Pull up the tarp."

After Hans rolled the tarp up, the guard jumped up and looked around the empty space.

The other guard ordered Hans to open the gas tank caps.

Hans took the cap off the tank not holding Karyn. The guard looked inside. "And the other cap, fool."

The other guard asked, "Are you planning to buy gas in the West?"

"No. I have plenty of gas."

"I can see that."

The guard took the papers from Hans into the guard house.

The other one said, "I think you are in trouble, Comrade."

Hans silently watched the other guard return from the guard house. "I cannot let you pass, Comrade. There is no record of your permit."

"I just got it this morning. It's probably not in the system. You know how slow it goes here."

"Yes, I know." He studied the permit, handed it back to Hans, and waved him into the American sector.

Hans got back in the truck and drove straight to a West Berlin garage controlled by the CIA. Agents closed the garage door as Hans stepped down from the cab and drained the gasoline before removing the top of the tank giving Karyn daylight for the first time in two hours.

Karyn stepped out. She stiffly, slowly stretched herself to stand upright.

Hans said, "We meet Josef here. He will take you to a safe place."

"And we must destroy the truck before the Soviets come here looking for it."

"You think that's possible?"

Hans answered, "The stasi will make the request because they can do it; I think the *volpi* at Checkpoint Charlie did not like the situation."

"The CIA has a way of making trucks disappear."

Josef and Karyn left the garage in his car. "You must go underground for a while," he explained.

When KGB Colonel Biroschnikov learned of Hans's truck entering the American sector through Checkpoint Charlie, he ordered stasi commander Holgar, "Send the Soviet representative there to find the truck, and when the driver returns to East Berlin, arrest and bring the traitor here for interrogation."

Holgar asked, "You think he will come back here?"

"Yes. It might be a connection to the priest, although I'm not sure what Hans will do. Now go."

Three hours later, Soviet agents returned and told Biroschnikov, "We found the burned truck in the West, and it was abandoned."

Biroschnikov asked, "Who owns it?"

His agent told him, "A woman in Chicago."

"That's impossible."

The other agent said, "The license plates were stolen from an East German truck."

"Any sign of the driver?" Biroschnikov inquired.

"No."

"For the sake of Lenin, find the son of a bitch."

Glasnost and Perestroika

A young man entered Holgar's office, escorted by Markus, his new assistant, who thereafter quickly went out and shut the door.

Holgar was annoyed by the interruption. "What do you want?"

"Comrade Holgar, I was a member of the colonel's youth troop. My name is Erik. Erik Shafer."

"Ah, yes. Shafer. I remember. What can I do for you?"

"The German Democratic Republic is doomed, because Moscow will never let us be free and independent."

"Thinking like that is treason. I can have you shot," Holgar reminded him.

Shafer told him, "But you won't. Listen to me. Our country is decaying. Our products don't match those of the West—"

Holgar stood and shouted, "Get out. I don't want to hear such shit."

"I can leave, but you cannot run from the facts. The young people will force changes in Germany. We have the chance now to break with Moscow."

"You are crazy."

Shafer asked, "Have you heard about Poland?"

"What about Poland?"

"Solidarity is now acceptable to the government. If Poland can become free, why can't our country?"

Holgar laughed. "The Poles will be crushed. A KGB officer was here this morning and said nothing of the kind. Your information is quite incorrect. Now get out."

Shafer smiled when he answered, "In no time the freedoms will come to us, Comrade Holgar. Germany will be reunited. Will you be ready for your new life?"

Holgar again shouted. "The party will never let reunification happen. Get out of my sight before I arrest you."

After Shafer left his office, Holgar sat silently pondering what he had just heard coming from the intercom system. Then he dialed a number. "Markus, get in here immediately."

Holgar asked his assistant, "What do you know about the rumor that the Polish youth are rebelling?"

"It is true. General Soviet and Party Secretary Gorbachev is encouraging freedom of expression and independence. It's called glasnost and perestroika. I think the wall will come down."

"Bullshit. The Polish police will crush the traitors."

"Gorbachev will forbid them to intervene."

Holgar raised his voice. "This cannot be."

"Make plans to be with the winners," Markus suggested, "and I would not wait if I were you."

Escape Over the Wall

A soldier stood at attention in front of Holgar's desk, behind which sat Holgar and Biroschnikov, who asked the soldier what he wanted.

"Comrade Leader, I have news about a planned escape over the wall.

It is the priest and his friends."

Holgar suddenly became interested, put down the document he was reading, and leaned forward to look at his guest. "Tell me all about it."

"My contacts tell me that next Monday a woman, a boy, and a man will go over the wall."

Biroschnikov told him, "We hear that all the time. Be specific, or get out."

"They plan to use Zone 3. The lights will be delayed to give them time to get away."

"Zone 3? How do you know the zone?"

The soldier told him, "I don't. My contacts said it would be Zone 3."

"Who's behind this plan?" Biroschnikov questioned.

"I don't know, Comrade. But I will report if I hear more."

Holgar got up from his chair and walked around to the front of the desk. He smiled at the soldier. "You did very well, Comrade. Tell my assistant your name so he can reward you." When the soldier didn't move, Holgar said loudly, "Now get out and let me plan strategy for dealing with this treachery."

The soldier told Holgar's assistant, Markus, what Holgar had said.

"You have done well, Comrade," Markus noted. "Your report is noted, and we will stop this attempt by traitors to leave our glorious country. It's another effort by the decadent CIA to kidnap three of our finest citizens."

He then wrote out a note and stamped it with Holgar's official stasi seal. Markus told the soldier, "Take this to your commanding officer. It is an order to give you extra food rations and Western cigarettes for one month."

The soldier saluted and said, "Thank you, Comrade. I am most grateful to serve our glorious country. Long live the German Democratic Republic."

"You are welcome, Comrade. Now go. I have work to do."

There Won't Be Any Trial

The next morning a solitary car moved along a deserted East German roadway near Potsdam. Inside were Holgar and his former assistant Franz. Early that morning three of Holgar's agents had arrested him and taken him to the Stasi headquarters where he had to wait in a jail cell. Forty-five minutes later Holgar took Franz, handcuffed, at gunpoint to an unmarked Stasi car.

Holgar said, "You betrayed me, Franz. That's treason, and the penalty is death."

Franz answered, "I am not afraid of the court system. After the judges hear what I have to say, you'll be tried and convicted for abuse of your power."

Holgar laughed as he spoke. "There won't be any trial, Franz After a thirty minute drive Holgar turned the car onto a desolate lane."

Franz asked, "What are we doing here?"

"I just want to have a secret talk with you."

The car stopped on a lonely lane in the middle of a dense Grove of Elm trees, a location that would be desired by lovers seeking privacy.

"Why should we have a secret talk?" Franz questioned.

"You'll find out," Holgar responded.

Holgar turned off the engine, and repositioned himself to face Holgar. The former assistant asked, "Are you going to really shoot me, Holgar?"

"No. I want you to tell me everything you know about Karyn, the priest, and the boy."

They exited the car and walked on the edge of the road.

Franz asked, "You really like her boy, don't you? What you do with the little boys when you are done with them is gruesome."

"Shut up. Cooperate and you won't die. Tell me how the bitch, her son, and her priest lover get over the wall?"

"I am not sure," he lied. "I was told there will be a mechanical failure with the lights."

"Is it true they will escape through Zone 3? Only a few people know there are no mines in that zone. You knew that."

"You are mistaken."

"Bullshit. You could have found out."

Franz shrugged. "How?"

"My informant told me that you are helping that whore bitch, her son, and the priest."

Franz laughed when he answered. "They want to leave."

"No one wants to voluntarily leave our glorious country, Comrade. The decadent Western agents lure the escapees to go over the wall. I know this for a fact because I am the Stasi."

Franz told him that only the privileged elite want to stay.

They continued walking in silence.

Franz told Holgar, "You have no proof we helped Karyn, the priest, and the boy. Your snitch tells you what you want to hear in order to gain favors and benefits. It's the corrupt system at work, Holgar. And you are the worst."

Holgar suddenly turned and shot Franz in the head. He grabbed his feet and dragged his former assistant's body into the wooded area where he had dug a hole earlier. He rolled the body into the hole and shoveled dirt to fill it.

Holgar muttered to himself. "*You are the one who's corrupt, Comrade. You are against the state. Now you cannot defile our glorious country. In the name of Comrade Lenin, I send you straight to hell.*"

You Were the Best

Holgar was standing behind his desk with a cigarette dangling from his lips when he casually responded to a knock on the door. "Come in." A young man entered, escorted by Markus. Surprised, Holgar asked, "Is that really you, Fleischer?" He then waved Markus out of the room.

"Yes."

"You've grown up, Son."

"Yes, my love," Fleischer said. "I have. How have you been?"

Fleischer was six foot three with a square jaw, a prominent nose, and piercing brown eyes that some say could look into a man's soul.

Holgar, pleased to see him again, asked. "Well, I thought you had forgotten me." He came around from behind his desk.

Fleischer smiled. "How could I? We had such good times in bed together. I am finished with the university at Leipzig."

"You were the best. I wonder what it will be like after all these years.Surely you can stay?"

"Let's find out, shall we?"

"Of course. Come with me." Holgar took Fleischer's hand and led him into his sleeping room adjacent to the office. The young man carried a small duffel bag.

They kissed on the lips, and as soon as he wrapped his arms around Fleischer, Holgar's breath began to come in rapid puffs. As Holgar bent over to draw back the sheets, Fleischer took a large knife from a sheath hidden inside his jacket. He quickly grabbed Holgar from behind, covered his mouth with his left hand, and stabbed him through the left side of his back into his heart, twisting the knife savagely like he was reaming out a pumpkin. Holgar tried to shout, but he made only a muffled sound through Fleischer's fingers. Fleischer pushed Holgar onto the bed facedown, pulled the knife out, cut the victims belt, and pulled Holgar's pants down to his ankles, revealing the bare white buttocks. Fleischer inserted the long knife blade into Holgar's rectum, reaming it savagely like one would do to remove burned tobacco from a pipe bowl. Blood gushed from his Holgar's anus.

Fleischer whispered "I hope you like it up the ass this time, lover."

Holgar tried to shout, but he was too weak as death overtook him.

Fleischer removed the knife, wiped it clean on the sheet, and replaced it in the sheath. He quickly changed into the fresh clothing he removed from his small duffel bag and stuffed his bloody clothing into it. He then looked around and slowly exited the office.

Fleischer came out of Holgar's office door and nodded to Markus who was sitting at the desk reading a man's magazine featuring photos of women's naked bodies.

"Comrade Holgar does not want to be disturbed," Fleischer said right before walking out of view.

Markus smiled knowingly and then returned to his magazine, put his hand down the front of his pants, played with himself all the while letting the pictures of nude German girls occupy his imagination.

Bullets Struck Close to Them

For some undisclosed reason, whoever laid out the Berlin Wall and the adjacent fence along the Spree River made a grave mistake. (Or was it a mistake?) The result was an area impossible for the soldiers in the guard towers to observe. It was then that the cloudy sky of nighttime over the east bank of the Spree River made it perfect for an underwater escape.

Jacob and Hans were in their scuba diving gear, crouched close to that part of the barrier fence on the edge of East Berlin not visible to the guards. Hans checked his watch and told the priest, "We have just three minutes to get into the water."

Hans used wire cutters to make a hole in the fence large enough to crawl through. Hans went first, and when the priest was through the fence, he reinstalled the cutout section.

At the edge of the river, the two slowly, noiselessly slipped into the dark water and vanished from sight beneath the surface.

Bright searchlight beams that customarily swept the river, stopped where the guards saw strange movement in the water surface and held there. Suddenly, machine-gun fire from a guard tower struck the turbulent surface of the river that was illuminated, the section beneath which were Hans and Jacob swimming.

The escapees swam four feet under the surface of the river. Bullets came harmlessly close to them as they continued at that depth to the western edge.

The pair ascended to the surface and prepared to climb onto the western bank when stray bullets found Jacob's back, left side, and legs. The shooting from the eastern side stopped when the shooters saw US soldiers standing on the western bank with weapons ready and pointed to the other side.

Members of the military group on the western bank helped Rolf pull Jacob and Hans up to the safety of the land. The East German guards stood quietly watching the activity, aware they could do nothing. Some wished they had made a swim like that but dare not speak of it.

As soon as one of the soldiers saw the blood on Jacob's wet suit, he called for the medic. They immediately cut off Jacob's diving gear straps and wet suit.

Hans slipped out of his diving gear and buoyancy jacket and then stripped off his wet suit. He and Jacob shivered from the cold of the night air. The medic covered Jacob with a blanket after examining his wounds and dressing them to stop the bleeding. He called for a stretcher from the ambulance.

"This man is in critical condition. Get him to the hospital quickly."

Karyn rushed from behind the crowd to Jacob. "Is he dead? Is he dead? Jacob darling, say something." She knelt next to Jacob, holding him as he lay inert, slowly breathing as medics lifted his body on to a gurney that they then rolled into the ambulance.

Paramedics inside checked Jacob over before closing the rear doors. Seconds before the ambulance was ready to rush away, code 3, Karyn banged her fist on the ambulance. She shouted, "Take me with you."

Murphy ordered the driver to take Karyn to the hospital.

"She's East German without papers," the driver pointed out. "I can take care of that. Just take her with you."

Hans towel dried his hair and body before stepping into a running suit. When he was handed a cup of hot coffee, he was told, "We won't know anything until the doctors have had a good look at Jacob's injuries. Right now his blood pressure is too low, and he's in shock."

Hans drank his coffee laced with cognac while watching the ambulance speed away to the hospital. Then he ate the ham sandwich he was offered.

Murphy of the CIA said, "Welcome to the West, Hans. Come with us."

He Is in Intensive Care

Karyn hugged her son, her eyes red from crying. She said a prayer of thanks that her son was well and that they were finally in the West. The US Army had delivered Jon to the West Berlin US Army hospital where he joined his mother in the emergency waiting room. She was awaiting word on Jacob's post-op condition.

Jon had been smuggled from East to West Berlin in the trunk of a Mercedes Benz bearing license plates registered to an East Berlin diplomat whom the resident CIA agent knew him well made the request.

A surgeon in blue disposable clothing, his mask hanging from his neck, approached. "I am Dr. Meier. Are you the next of kin?"

Karyn told him, "No, but a close friend. He has no family here. He's an American priest."

"A priest?"

"Yes. Will Father Gorska live?"

He answered, "We are doing all that we can. He's been severely—I'd even say gravely—wounded. He had six bullets in his body. One narrowly missed his heart but nicked an artery, and another pierced his lung. We stopped the bleeding and inflated the lung, and he's breathing normally on a ventilator. His vitals look much better after surgery."

Karyn wiped her eyes. "Where is he? Can I see him?"

"No visitors, because he's in the intensive care ward on oxygen and life support."

Murphy of the CIA entered the room and introduced himself. "Can you tell us about his wounds?"

Dr. Meier repeated what he had told Karyn.

"What can we do?"

"Nothing at this point. Go home and get your rest. Pray for him. Wait for the daily progress reports."

"But can I stay near him in case he needs me?" Karyn asked.

"As you wish, Karyn. I'll order a reclining chair and blanket be brought into a vacant room for you. Feel free to use our cafeteria."

You Want to Start Another War?

Ryan Litchfield patiently waited in the lobby of the CIA West Berlin Operations Base office (BOB) station. A US Marine corporal at the front desk read the card she handed him.

"I don't understand your visit, Miss Litchfield."

"I am an American investigative journalist from the *New York Times* and the *International Herald Tribune* in Paris." She showed him her press pass but refused to give it to him when he asked for it, knowing there was a chance she would not get it back without trouble.

"So what can I do for you, Miss Litchfield?"

"I am writing a report about Father Jacob Gorska. I have questions about his escape."

"Please come with me," the corporal directed. After she was seated across the desk from him, he told her, "We know of no such Father Jacob Gorska."

She said, "What can you tell me about the attempted murder?"

"There again, I must ask. What attempted murder?"

"Are you sure you have no file on Father Jacob Gorska? I think Mr. Murphy who is in charge here will know what I am talking about."

The soldier stepped around his desk. "Please wait here. And do not do any snooping. You'll find nothing worthwhile."

She smiled. "I promise. Scout's honor," she said as she crossed her heart.

He flashed her a cynical smile and left the room.

Soon, an army captain holding a file entered the area motioned for her to follow him into another room. He sat at the desk and set down a folder bearing on the cover large red letters spelling out the words: TOP SECRET.

"My name is Captain Buckley of the US Army Intelligence Department. The person you earlier talked with knows nothing of what you speak."

Ryan smiled. "But you do?"

"All I know is in this file. How do you fit in with the priest?"

"I am a very good friend."

"How good a friend?" Buckley smiled with a near leer.

"We grew up together."

"Ah, I see. But now you write stories for the IHT."

"I write reports about current events."

"Whatever you say." Buckley opened the folder, read the cover page, and said, "Father Gorska was shot by East Berlin police while swimming the Spree River in order to get from East to West Berlin. He is lucky to be alive."

Ryan quickly said, "He successfully swam to the west side and was shot while getting out of the river? I think it was a case of attempted murder."

"I don't think he quite made it that far when he was shot."

"But he was in the West German area of the river. Right?"

"So are you trying to expose the atrocities of the East Berlin police?" Captain Buckley questioned.

"What are the facts that you have?"

He explained, "All we know is that a man who said he was a priest and another East German man swam across the Spree River from east to west. The priest was shot just as he was about to reach the West German bank."

Ryan said, "How can the Soviets who control one part of Berlin enforce everyone's travel restrictions in violation of the postwar agreements that determined what countries would occupy separate parts of the city?"

Buckley laughed. "Come on. This has been the case for almost forty years. You think you can untangle this mess? You want to start another war?"

"Who said there would be a war? I don't think Moscow wants a war."

Buckley explained how the United States, Britain, France, and the USSR have been negotiating through their diplomatic representatives to ease travel to the West.

Ryan stood and told Buckley, "I guess I'll just have to talk with the East German police then."

"I doubt they will talk to you about this matter. You are American. To them, you are evil and depraved."

It was Ryan's turn to laugh. She said, "They're not the only ones who think that. Thanks for your help."

She shook hands with Buckley. On her way to the hospital, she made a request for a meeting with the East Berlin Police.

Fifty-Fifty Today

When Ryan Litchfield entered the hospital room, she saw Susan Ralls and her husband, Ted Fontaine, standing beside the bed. Jacob was asleep, his right arm hooked up to an IV drip and a machine connected by wires to his chest that was monitoring vital signs. Oxygen flowed through cannulas in his nose.

Susan told Ryan it was good seeing her again. They hugged. Ryan hugged Ted.

"Are you still living in Paris?" Susan asked.

"Yes."

"Are you working in Berlin?"

"Yes. I am writing about Jacob's escape."

Ted asked, "And are you getting true answers to your questions?"

"Not easily," Ryan answered. "But I am persistent."

Karyn entered the room, and Ted introduced her to Ryan.

There was a pause before Ryan told Karyn, "It's good to meet you after all these years. Jacob talked so much with me about you." She sat in a chair next to Karyn. "From what Jacob told me, I feel I already know you."

"How do you know him?"

Ryan smiled. "We grew up together as teenagers in Michigan."

There was a knock on the door before it opened slowly. Dr. Reiner Meier walked in. The surgeon introduced himself and shook hands around the room before reading the nurses' notes in the chart at the foot of Jacob's bed.

Ted asked, "What is the prognosis, Doctor?"

The physician glanced up. "Fifty-fifty today. That's better than yesterday, and I hope worse than tomorrow."

Susan wiped the tears from her face and said, "So it looks like Jacob will make it?"

"Let's hope so. He's not fully out of danger, but he's headed toward recovery mode. His body was badly torn up, but he had it in his favor that he was in very good physical condition—more so than most priests I have met. I've seen experienced combat soldiers in poorer condition survive."

Susan held Ted close and cried on his shoulder.

As the doctor was leaving the room, Father Mickey McFarland walked in.

Dr. Meier said, "I'll leave you all to chat. Don't stay longer than fifteen minutes. Father Gorska needs much quiet time for the next five days."

Father McFarland told the group, "Jacob has to survive."

Ted asked, "His mission was not accomplished?"

"Until Communism is defeated, Jacob has an important role to play."

Susan said, "Surely he's not going back to Poland."

McFarland answered, "That's where he's needed."

Ted said, "He's critically wounded. Surely that is enough."

"Getting Karyn and Jon out of East Berlin was foolish," said Father McFarland. "That was not his mission. He disobeyed orders. For this, God has punished him."

Karyn began to cry.

Ted told the priest, "That's bullshit, Father."

"I realize why you are angry, but God works in strange ways. It's really a decision for Pope John Paul II to make. Let us pray for Jacob's speedy recovery."

The group bowed their heads as Father McFarland led them in prayer.

What About Biroschnikov?

Ryan was refused access to East Berlin officials but received permission to visit the CIA station chief in West Berlin, Brad Murphy. She thanked him for talking with her.

"You said on the phone you had some interesting news," Ryan said.

Murphy opened a file folder and removed a sheet of paper. He slid it across his desk to Ryan and said, "This is classified. In your case, you need to know this information if you really want to pursue this investigation. This information must be off the record and cannot be published."

Ryan studied the paper. "What is this?"

"The East German ballistics report of the tests made on Holgar's Walther semiautomatic 9 mm pistol. It shows that the bullet taken from Agent Franz's body matches the bullets taken from the bodies of Jacob's parents."

The news surprised Ryan. "The police have the bullets taken from them all those years ago?"

Murphy smiled. "That's the wonderful thing about Russian intelligence precision in Communist Poland. Nothing goes unrecorded."

"Was this Biroschnikov's gun?"

"Yes, according to government records."

"If Biroschnikov had this gun in 1949, then how did Holgar get it?"

"I guess when the KGB upgraded weapons, they gave the old weapons to the poor cousins in East Berlin."

Ryan asked for the source of Murphy's information.

Murphy smiled. "Now that is something you don't have a right to know. I must protect my sources in East Berlin."

"So it is a report from the East Berlin secret police?"

"I can't say, but it is as if they provided it."

"Are you saying the West and East intelligence agencies work together?" asked Ryan.

Murphy nodded. "On occasion, when it helps both sides. We try to work with each other on major crimes because both sides know the bad guys run back and forth across the zones and must be captured. Events are finally changing behind the Iron Curtain."

Ryan asked, "So will East Berlin prosecute?"

"Who is there to prosecute?"

"I don't understand."

"Holgar was found murdered in his bed," he explained. "His gun is another confirmation of events. Case closed."

"What about the killer of Jacob's parents?" she asked.

"The KGB protects its own. I doubt Biroschnikov will be prosecuted."

"How can you be sure that Biroschnikov is the one who murdered Jacob's parents?"

The CIA agent explained to her that the Polish, Soviet, and East German secret police had a sterling intelligence operations record. "And besides Jacob remembered the murderer had a scarlet birthmark on his face, the same as Biroschnikov."

"So who killed Holgar?"

Murphy shrugged. "Who cares?"

Epilogue

In her last report of Jacob's mission, Ryan Litchfield wrote the following:

Father Jacob Gorska survived with minor residual results that affect his walking, and notwithstanding them, he accepted an assignment of the pope to carry more messages from Rome and President Reagan to Lech Walesa, whom he met in Budapest. He made three additional trips to Hungary, where he met with Polish partisans. He was later assigned to the Jesuit's office of the order's superior general in Rome, which worked closely with the Vatican secretary of state negotiating security for priests in Poland.

On June 12, 1987, President Reagan visited West Berlin and on a platform overlooking the wall into the East Berlin addressed the cheering crowd in front of the Brandenburg Gate. He was advised not to, but he altered his prepared speech and loudly said to the crowd, "Mr. Gorbachev, tear down this wall." His remarks were met with thundering applause.

November 9, 1989, saw the first East Berlin citizens attack the Berlin Wall, which was eventually torn down by young citizens on both sides. Hundreds of people on both sides of the Berlin Wall with picks and hammers assaulted the symbol of the oppressive Soviet regime, which had lasted for twenty-eight years.

Shortly after the wall was partially opened with enough room to squeeze through, hundreds of East Berliners like an avalanche rushed into West Berlin without restriction.

The USSR was officially dissolved December 26, 1991, at which time the former Soviet Republics were made independent. Replacing the Soviet Union was the newly created Russian Commonwealth of Independent States (CIS). These events resulted in the end of the Cold War and the disappearance of the Iron Curtain.

The general secretary of the Communist Party at the time, Mikhail Gorbachev, the eighth and last leader of the Soviet Union as Soviet president, declared his office extinct and resigned. Boris Yeltsin became the leader of the nation.

East Germany was united with West Germany as a free democratic nation.

Lech Walesa received the 1983 Nobel Peace Prize. Also in 1989, Poland's Solidarity Party was recognized with Lech Walesa as its leader. He ran for office and was elected president of Poland.

Karyn and Jon moved to a small town in Northern California with a pension provided by the new German government.

Father Mickey McFarland taught classes at the Jesuit High School and Academy in Detroit. He died in Chicago as a result of a heart attack in 1992 while visiting his family.

Ted and Susan Ralls-Fontaine built a six-thousand-square-foot home in Belvedere on the San Francisco Bay, where they enjoy sailing their forty-five-foot sailboat called *the Wizard*. They often have Karyn and Jon as guests. Jon attended University of California at Santa Barbara, where he studied political science.

On occasion, Hans, the man who drove Karyn in the truck gas tank through Checkpoint Charlie to the West, often visits Karyn and her son.

Ryan Litchfield continued her investigative reporting freelance for several magazines.

Poland was restored to its independent status.

Pope John Paul II visited his native Poland, where he was given thundering ovations.

President Reagan served out his second and last term before he left the White House in 1989.